TO LOVE AND SECOND CHANCES

VIOLET HAZE

Dear Reader,

In 2014, I published *Refuge* and then the follow-up *Revive* two years later. *Refuge* was the first novella I wrote and published. I've been meaning to give this story a facelift for a couple years now. I believe the story will be better enjoyed as one novel instead of split into two, plus I love the new cover. It is gorgeous and more fitting to the great love story between Evie & Dominick!

I've loved this story since the moment I wrote it and although I've edited it and changed some of the wording (since my writing skills have improved over time), the story hasn't changed nor was anything added because after reading it through, this love story is perfect as-is.

Happy reading!
<3 Violet

CHAPTER 1

I stabbed him!

Oh god, I stabbed him.

I stumble toward the car, the one that brought us both up here.

Oh god.

I look over my shoulder, but he isn't chasing me.

I didn't kill him, did I?

I didn't even check. I just ran.

I hope he isn't dead.

I press the unlock key, the beeping of the car hurting my already sensitive ears, and wince. I open the door and slide behind the wheel.

He never lets me drive the car.

He'll be upset when he catches me.

I know it's when and not if.

But maybe... maybe if I drive fast enough, I can get somewhere to ditch the car?

I didn't want to kill him.

I just wanted out.

Out. Out. Out.

Turning the key, it starts easily. After putting it in drive, I hit the gas and the car jerks.

Okay, it's been a while.

I let out the sigh of relief I've been holding as the cabin disappears in my rearview mirror.

And then a scream.

The last thing I feel is fear as the car goes airborne.

But it's not fear that I'll die.

It's despair of what will happen if I don't.

CHAPTER 2

"Tell me about these dreams."

I've already told him about them many times.

The doctor scribbles on his page behind me.

Is it weird I don't know what my doctor looks like?

He claims it's because he's such a good-looking man, he has to keep what he looks like a secret. Otherwise, the patients — male and female, he's informed me — fall in love with him. Already had that happen once or twice, y'know? He'd said that.

And when he told me that, of course I laughed, but gossip around the psych ward is he's telling the truth.

I suppose I can believe it.

He's got one of those voices that oozes charm, and patience, and kindness, and sexiness.

I bet he's real hot, but I can't verify it because like I said, he won't let me see him at all.

That's okay, though since I see him in my dreams. I wish I had knowledge of his looks, but I guess that's the good thing about not. I can make him up to how I see him, and ensure his voice say all the dirty things I wish it would say... and well, guess it's all I'll get and I should be happy with it.

"Zee?"

I wince.

That's not my name.

Would you believe I don't know my name?

Apparently, a car accident three months ago took my memory. All of it.

I don't know my name, my age, or where I came from.

They said the car they found me in was registered to a fake name.

A fake person. How the fuck is that even possible?

They asked me a bunch of questions, even where I'd been driving to or from, and nothing.

A big, fat, fucking nothing.

So he calls me Zee, because... well, because I didn't like any other letter of the alphabet.

I dunno why. Z seemed rather fitting for someone who doesn't know their name or anything else.

It's the end of the alphabet and often forgotten.

Like I'm forgotten since it doesn't seem as if anyone is looking for me.

That's okay, though.

I get to stay here in a room that's always quiet at night, with three meals a day, therapy, some music, and where I've come to feel as if I belong.

Okay, okay, perhaps I'm crazy.

Hey, I am in a psych ward and if you can't beat them, join them. Right?

Wait, where did I hear that before?

"Zee? Focus."

"Oh." I blush as his hand touches my shoulder. "Sorry."

His hand is the only body part I've seen of him.

God, he's got nice hands.

I dream about them touching me. All over.

All fucking over.

This isn't right!

"S-sex dreams." The words come out as a stutter. Why do I stutter when I say sex? It's like I'm afraid.

Afraid of what?

I don't know.

"I don't know! I don't fucking know!"

"Zee. Breathe." His hand is steady on my shoulders. "Deep breath in." A pause. "Good. Now out."

Yes, in and out.

That's exactly what I want him to do to me.

I laugh, and he sighs, sitting back and therefore removing his touch. "Zee. Why do you think you keep having these dreams?"

"I think it's your voice. It's comforting. Safe."

"It's not appropriate to have those sorts of dreams about me."

"Nothing is actually appropriate in a psych ward, is it?"

"Zee."

"You enjoy saying my name, don't you? That's okay. I say your name a lot in my dreams."

He says nothing. Doesn't even sigh.

Is this guy made of stone?

I mean, I know I'm a psych patient, but there's no chance he doesn't find me attractive.

I'm the prettiest patient here, and I'm not just saying that.

I win the beauty pageants the other patients throw every single time.

Okay, I suppose that's weird.

"Do you think I'll be this way this forever, Doc?"

"No."

"Why not?"

"You are afraid of something. I believe when we figure out what you're afraid of, everything else will fall into place." He writes something down again and then asks, "Whose blood was on you, Zee? It wasn't yours, and you didn't have a scratch on you other than from your head hitting the steering wheel."

"How did that even happen? They said I flipped that car."

This is like the ten-thousandth time we've discussed this, but I still don't get it.

Lucky, I'm so lucky.

That's what they tell me.

Whatever.

If I'm so lucky, why am I in a psych ward?

Yah. They can never answer that particular question.

"Whose was it?"

He always ignores my question, and repeats his own, as if the answer will suddenly change.

"I dunno, Doc. It's all a blank."

"Perhaps the car was really yours?"

"No." I don't know why I'm so adamant, but that car wasn't mine. "No, it wasn't mine. I know — know — that much. I was escaping."

"From who? From where?"

I bring my hands up to my ears and cover them, the words getting louder and louder as my ears ring, and I scream.

Soon, I'm back in my room, all alone.

And I still don't know what the doctor looks like.

CHAPTER 3

I STRETCH AS THE HEATED SAND CRADLES MY FEET, slipping in between my toes as I wiggle them, and toss him a glance.

Shading his eyes with his hand, he grins up at me from his seat on the blanket, the warmth and richness of his voice rolling over me. "You like the view?"

"Like it?" I sit on the blanket beside him and hug him with a squeal of delight. "I love it! I could stay here forever."

He chuckles, sliding his hands around my midsection and resting his hands on my back, tugging me close as he captures my lips with his.

Mm. His mouth is divine and always has been. From the moment we met, I knew we would kiss, and it would be perfection.

And it had been. Still is.

He gives the kind of kisses that make me feel even when I don't want to.

Truth is, he's the only person who has ever made me feel anything, and sometimes, that's terrifying. He has such power over me, and the moment he figures it out...

"You're distracted." He pulls his lips away, his words dragging me from my thoughts to once again gazing into his eyes. "What're you thinking about?"

"Your kissing skills. They're amazing."

He throws his head back and laughs, and I can't help admiring him.

He's six foot, with chocolate brown hair, and eyes so dark they look black. The golden quality to his skin makes me jealous, because he never burns, merely gets this lovely tan so many women would be envious of. He's muscular, but not in a crazy sort of way, and even though he carries himself in an indolent manner, he's anything but lazy.

And he's all mine and has been for over a year.

Distracted as he is, I tackle him to the ground on this empty beach with its warm sand and hot sunlight, and nip the lobe of his ear.

"Always playful," he murmurs, crushing our mouths together for a second, stealing my breath as he rolls over on top of me and laughs. "You know I'm always up for getting naked on the beach."

One hand skims my bare leg, the other slips around my neck to untie the straps keeping my bikini top on, and once loosened, he pulls them down to bare my breasts. Cupping one in his hand, he smiles at me, his eyes shining as he asks, "When are you going to tell me?"

I arch into his hand, aching for his touch, and my eyelids flutter shut. "Tell you what?"

"You're pregnant?"

"N-no, I'm not." I try to scuttle away, but his body traps mine, and he frowns at my denial. "Why would you say that?"

"Why do you look so frightened?" He takes his hand off my breast and tucks a piece of stray hair behind my ear, the grin on his face widening. "I've been enjoying you and your gorgeous breasts for more than a year now. I think I'd notice they've gotten bigger."

I look down at my chest with confusion.

Have they gotten bigger? I hadn't thought anything of it.

"You look... happy."

Why do I sound confused at his happiness? Maybe it's because I should've noticed first.

When was my last period, anyway?

"Why wouldn't I be happy?" He cuts into my thoughts with a peck on the lips. "I love you. A baby with you would make me even happier."

"I... I didn't know." My voice is urgent, as if I'm trying to convince him I'm not lying, but it's not as if he's accusing me of lying.

What the hell is wrong with me?

"Hey, sweetheart, calm down. I guess you just weren't paying attention." He chuckles, covering my lips with his hungry ones, and sweeps all thoughts from my mind as he makes love to me.

I'm so lucky.

CHAPTER 4

Sleeping.

It's bedtime, and asleep in my bed is where I should be, but I'm tiptoeing to my Doc's office instead.

The door is cracked as I approach, and I hide because there's another person in there with him.

A female.

My instinct is to hiss, yet I don't. Why would I, though? It's not like I own him, but she's probably looking at him and I don't even get to look at him.

"No luck?" The woman says and Doc, the man with the hot voice and even hotter hands, growls with frustration and makes her laugh. "I'm sorry. I know it's rough."

"She's totally gone. There is nothing left."

She? Who is she?

"She isn't getting any better?"

"No." I hear a glass tap, almost as if he's setting it down on a table, and then a chair creak, which tells me he's sitting at his desk. "She doesn't know anything, remember anything. It's like... it's like she's locked it all up inside."

"She doesn't even know you're her husband?"

What? He has a wife?

Sharp pinpricks in my chest have me holding my hand up to my chest, and one fist up to my mouth to stifle my increased breathing.

"Hardly. She won't even look at me. She just lays there."

Sounds like a frigid bitch. Okay, okay, that might be disingenuous. After all, sounds like his wife has completely gone nuts. Poor guy.

"What will you do?"

"Simple. Perhaps I should take her home. Try going for shock value." He laughs, but it's humorless. Poor him. He sounds pitifully sad. "Might work, may have me bringing her back here to lock up for good."

Oh. His wife is here.

I immediately go through all the other patients his wife could be and come up with a few I shall question. I'll find his wife and tell her he's going to lock her up for good if she doesn't cooperate. After all, she gets to see his face, and I don't. And I'll tell her if she doesn't want him, I'll take him.

Heaven knows I've dreamt enough about him and me naked lately.

Mmm.

I turn around and head back to bed as they start talking about boring stuff.

I'll get to see the Doc tomorrow. I see him every day, much to the dismay of the other patients, but that's not my problem.

I obviously need more help than they do.

Especially since I have two therapists.

CHAPTER 5

Someone's sitting in a chair in my room.

It's dark, but I woke up and there they are, just sitting there.

Then, the delicious smell of his cologne reaches me, and I smile.

"Doc. You're not supposed to be in my room."

"I'm not Doc. Why do you call me that?"

I know we can barely see each other, but I tilt my head anyway, confused. "Yes, you are. Your voice... you're the voice of my doctor." I giggle, and he shifts in his chair, continuing to stare at me, not commenting.

I know he's staring at me, because I can feel it. I'm hyperaware, and it feels like his gaze burns me.

His eyes burn me, and his voice sets me on fire, and I wiggle under the blankets as my body revs to life. I imagine him touching me, and I want him to give in, so I try my best.

"You should come join me in bed. It's comfy and I'm all alone."

"I won't fall for that again."

My lower lip sticks out in a pout, and I pat the bed beside me. "Fall for what? I want you in bed with me. You can touch me with those hands of yours. I love your hands."

"I wish that were true."

I don't understand.

"I know," he says, and I'm sure he's reading my thoughts until I realize no, I said that out loud and he responded. "I know all too well."

And he gets up out of his chair, and comes over to the bed, and I still can't see his face.

But he leans over and kisses me on the forehead, and tears slide down my cheeks.

"I'm sorry," he says as he leaves the room, shutting the door behind him softly, and I cry harder.

Why is he sorry?

Why do I care?

What is wrong with me?

I wish I knew.

CHAPTER 6

"Z IS FOR ZANDER. YES, Z FITS YOU TO A TEE. TEN fingers, ten toes, Zander is precious and my little sweet pea!"

"If you're not careful, he'll grow up singing made up jingles," he says, coming up behind me and kissing my shoulder, as he smiles down at the baby before walking away.

I pick up Zander, who coos and grabs strands of my hair, shoving it in his mouth as he chants, "mama" over and over. I glance down at him, and his chubby eight month face stares back at me, adoration for me and my tasty red hair clear on his face. He smiles at me, chanting "mama mama" louder. When I laugh, he giggles and starts flailing, pulling my hair along with it.

"Ow! Zander, you're hurting mommy!"

I bring him closer to my body, holding him with one

arm and hand, while prying my hair free from his fist with the other.

Of course, he wails, and then he's taken from my arms so his father can distract him by holding him up in the air.

"Don't you cry. You can't pull on your mom's hair; no you can't!" He snuggles Zander close then, and nuzzles his nose, before looking at me and winking. "I'll lie him down for his nap. Why don't you rest a bit, hmm?"

"You always know what to do," I say with a weak smile, feeling tired suddenly. "He doesn't like me."

"Sure he does, sweetheart." Giving me a sweet kiss on the lips, Zander chants "ma ma" repeatedly, and his father raises his brows as he pulls his mouth away. "See? He doesn't say, 'dada' at all, so he obviously likes you best."

Then, with another wink and a dazzling smile, he's leaving the room to put Zander in his crib.

I grab the monitor, going over to the couch and stretching out on it, the last thing I hear before falling asleep the sound of my son babbling, and his father laughing.

CHAPTER 7

"WHAT'S YOUR NAME?"

"I don't know."

My second therapist — the one who lets me look at him — frowns at me. His hair is all grey, and he looks so tired. I only see him twice a week, and I much prefer my other therapist who puts his hand on my shoulder, trying to comfort me, and sees me every day with his smiling voice.

This guy merely seems annoyed with me, as if he wishes I'd hurry and remember who I am.

"What would you do if someone came here looking for you, telling you who you are, and taking you home?"

I move my gaze to stare out the window, unable to handle the look on his face; the one which is full of pity mingled with intense interest in my answer.

"I don't know. I like it here."

"Why? This isn't living. You are merely existing here. You can't stay here forever."

"I can't?"

"No. You don't belong here. You aren't mentally ill."

"How am I not? I can't remember anything."

"That's amnesia, Zee, and it's from your head trauma."

I shake my head, holding my hands up to my ears to block out his words, screaming, "No! No, it's not!"

"You're afraid of reality." His words are deliberately soft, so I have to listen. "There is no swelling on your brain, no permanent damage. You were escaping, you say, so you're afraid of something. What's locking you up, hmm? Why don't you want to go home?"

"Stop! Stop!"

Suddenly, I'm lying down and there he is. His hand is on my shoulder, and his lovely voice fills my ears with its joy. But I also hear his sadness; I feel it.

"This isn't working anymore." His hand squeezes my shoulder. "You don't seem to be improving here."

"You make things better. I don't like that other doctor. He's... he's mean."

When he chuckles behind me, I feel an immense happiness at making him do something rather than sigh at me in frustration, and I put my hand over his hand.

I feel him jump as if the contact is unexpected.

I guess I haven't touched him before.

Weird, since I feel like I've touched him a thousand times.

Then again, I think that's mostly in my dreams where we're touching each other inappropriately.

"Are you married?" The instinct to ask takes over my caution in knowing I shouldn't ask, because he's the one who's supposed to ask the questions. "Have a family?"

He clears his throat, pulling his hand out from under mine, and asks, "What makes you ask such a thing? You've never been curious before."

"I am now."

Can't tell him I heard him. I wasn't supposed to be out of bed. Don't want to get in trouble.

"Yes, I'm married."

"To a man or a woman?"

He laughs at my question, his hand coming back to rest on my shoulder, but I don't dare touch him for fear he'll pull away again. "A woman. Her name is Evie."

"Ah." Her name sounds familiar, but I must've seen it in a magazine or something. "And what about kids?"

"I had a son." He removes his hand and lets out a heavy sigh. "My wife didn't take his death too well."

"I'm sorry."

I'm not just saying that to him. I truly am sorry. His wife must've lost it after that.

Poor woman.

"Me too."

He says nothing else, and I guess he leaves, but I'm not sure because I think I passed out.

How rude of me.

CHAPTER 8

I don't know what wakes me, but the darkening sky through the gap in the curtains tells me I slept longer than I meant to.

And it's quiet.

So quiet.

Where is Zander?

Picking up the monitor and my phone, I head toward his room as I look down at the time.

Seven-oh-one.

The time sticks in my brain.

Three hours since he went down for a nap.

He has never slept this long.

I enter his room, and I see his form lying in the crib, and even across the room as I am, I know something is wrong.

I rush over and pick up my son.

Then I scream, and scream.

My fingers fumble to dial, but I finally manage it once my screams turn into moans of agony.

"Nine-one-one."

"Please, help me. My baby. My baby is dead!"

The lady speaks, but all I see is my precious Zander.

He's so cold and I know he's been dead long enough there is no reviving him.

I'll never see his beautiful dark brown eyes, so like his father's, ever again.

Where's his father?

Why isn't he here?

I start screaming his name, but he doesn't come.

Then I remember he told me he had to return to work and would be home late, words he'd woken me up to whisper before pressing a kiss on my lips, and telling me to get some more rest.

And so I wait, all alone, holding and rocking my baby, for what seems like eternity until there are people rushing into the room and leading us to the ambulance.

Someone asks me if there is anyone they can call for me. I don't even know who asks, but I hand them my phone and let them figure it out as we arrive at the hospital and I sit there as they take my baby away.

I don't know why. I know he's dead. They know he's dead.

How long I wait... I'll never know.

But then he comes through the doors and straight toward me.

And the moment he touches me, I lose it.

"Don't touch me!" He drops his hand, his eyes going wide, as I hold my hands up and step back. "This is all your fault!" I'm screaming and people are staring at me; the screaming only escalates as he tries to take me in his arms and I smack at him with my hands. "He's dead. He's dead because of you. You put him to bed and you were adamant I take a nap. What did you do? What did you fucking do?"

"Evie—"

"Don't! Don't say my name. And don't say his name." I cover my ears and sink to the floor, shaking my head as he says my name again, and a horrible wailing reaches my ears.

And as the sound gets louder and louder, I realize I'm the one making that horrible fucking noise, and I can't stop.

CHAPTER 9

I N THE PSYCH WARD, ONE OF THE MANY THINGS THEY make you do is activities. I know it's mostly a time filler. After all, you can't do therapy all day long, even if you have gorgeous doctors whose faces you never see.

You can pick from many, but the one I like best is painting.

I've been looking for the perfect spot to paint from. I've tried my room, the windows which look out into the park, and the center of the room with everyone around me.

But it seems no matter which spot I pick, none of them enable me to paint anything except what looks like it's supposed to be a baby. I can't seem to get his features right though, and even though I don't think we're supposed to paint a certain thing, it's the only thing I want to paint.

And I can't figure out why.

Difference is today... I know his eye color.

I mix the colors until it's just right, and even though it isn't perfect, on the page in front of me are two little beautiful dark brown eyes staring back at me.

Then I'm angry.

He's not just two eyes, dammit.

I mix more colors, and as if I'm suddenly looking at a photograph of a child, the strokes of my brush turn into something more, and soon... the eyes are on a beautiful little chubby face which smiles at me. I gasp at the pain shuddering through my chest as I recognize who it is.

Zander.

The pallet and brush slip from my fingers, and as it hits the floor and paint splatters, I put my face in my hands and start sobbing as I fall to my knees.

In moments, I'm gathered in someone's arms.

They seem so familiar, and when he speaks, his voice is instant comfort through the pain even though the tears still stream down my face, which is still buried in my hands and against his chest. "I've got you. Let's get you to your room."

I know everyone around me is staring, and as I feel him turn to head toward my room, he says, "Nobody touches that picture."

Something in his voice has me wondering why he cares, but before I can even think about it, he's laying me on my bed, and wrapping me in his arms, where I fall asleep with my head cradled against his chest.

And when I awaken, he's gone.

CHAPTER 10

"Do you know who Zander is?"

I'm in the office with the therapist I don't like, and he's looking at me with so much hope, but I'm in a bad mood today. I feel like dashing all his hopes because I can't take out my annoyance on the other one.

"No. It was just a picture, for fuck's sake."

"You said you've been trying to paint the baby for a while now, Zee."

I shrug, crossing my arms and cradling my stomach, gazing out the window as always, only this time I feel like rocking. I haven't wanted to rock in a long time.

The therapist is talking to me more, but I'm ignoring him.

Where is Doc?

It's been three days since he picked me up off the ground, and I usually see him every day.

Doesn't he know how much I need him?

Nobody will tell me where he is. They all look at me like I'm insane when I ask where the hot doctor nobody may look at went.

"I know your name, Zee."

At those words, I whip my head to face him, pointing a finger at him, and yell, "No!"

He lifts a brow, placing his pen down on the desk, before steepling his fingers and smiling. "Why don't you want to hear it?"

"You can't know my name. Nobody knows who I am."

"What if I said we do?" Even though I shake my head, he continues with whatever he thinks he has to say. "We were hoping you'd remember on your own. You've been through a lot in the last year before the accident, so we thought maybe you simply needed a break. But now I know you're afraid to know anything at all."

"Shut up!" I stand up and slam my hands down on his desk, glaring at him. "You shut up, right now!"

He sits back in his chair, unafraid, and puts his hands behind his head as he asks, "What does the name Dominick mean to you, Zee?"

"Don't say his name." I'm shouting now, shaking with the fear, anger, and grief speeding through me, and I back away toward the door. "Don't say either of their names, and don't say my name, and don't you—don't you—I... I want a new doctor."

"You're not getting a new doctor. You're going home in a few hours." He pauses, his mouth turning down in a frown as if he's sad for me, and then the corner of his mouth goes up in a ghost of a smile. "Being here isn't doing you any good. You should be with your husband... Evie."

"Screw you!" I shout, yanking open the door to showcase my anger more and almost sending myself tumbling back as the inside of my head pounds. When I can finally manage to pass through, I take off running toward my room.

I can't lock it behind me, but the satisfaction of slamming it gives me a temporary feeling of control as I collapse on my bed and curl into a ball.

CHAPTER 11

One year.

One whole year since our son died and he walks around like nothing has happened.

I don't even know if he remembers what today is, as he walks past me, kisses me on the cheek before saying goodbye, and heads out to work.

And just like every other day, I burst into tears the moment I know I'm safe from his overwhelming attention, because I know I'm getting on his nerves. It's been a year, and everyone thinks I should just move on, but my grief is so deep most days I can't breathe.

Rationally, I know it's not his fault.

It's not anyone's fault.

Zander died of SIDS.

Neither of us did anything wrong, but I blame him,

and he knows it. It doesn't matter that I shouldn't; that's the reality of our situation.

We haven't had sex since a month after Zander died, when Dominick — I guess searching for some semblance of normalcy — turned over in bed and took my perpetually sobbing form in his arms, and tried to seek solace in me.

And I, trying to comfort my husband even through my anger, couldn't muster much effort except to lie there as he did his thing.

It was the last time he approached me, and the only time we touch is when he says goodbye in the morning.

He puts his hand on my shoulder while standing behind me, then leans in and kisses me on the cheek, murmuring, "I love you. See you after work," every day without fail.

I can't even look at him.

And, for me, every day he does it, just shoves the knife deeper and deeper because I know he doesn't mean it.

I know he wishes he were rid of me too.

So, I will give him what he wants.

I make a few phone calls, and when he walks through the door at five, I'm standing there all dressed up and beam at him. His step falters and he stops walking as he stands a few feet away from me, a quizzical look on his face.

"Evie. Are you all right?" He lifts his hand, his thumb pointing back over his shoulder as he frowns. "Whose car is that in the driveway?"

"Mine. A rental." I walk over and past him, opening the door and indicating he should get in the car. "I wanted to take a night away. I've got our stuff in the car already."

His eyebrows fly up in surprise, which he quickly masks with a smile, and then nods. "All right. Sounds like a great plan to me. I'm glad you're feeling better."

"I'm driving," I say as we walk to the car and he shrugs, getting in the passenger side.

It's not until we're almost there that he notices something isn't right.

Perhaps it's because as we go around the curves of the road which leads to the cabin, I am going fast enough he needs to grab onto the handle, but it's too late.

When we pull up to the place — the one where we stayed to enjoy the beach for a few days, and the same place where he realized I was pregnant before I did — his face goes ashen, and I know he's remembered now what fucking day it is.

"Oh shit," he says as I climb out of the car and stalk toward the house, but he gets out and follows me, and I hit the lock button when his door shuts so he can't get back in. "Evie—"

"Don't you fucking dare!" I whirl around while standing in the doorway to the house, and point a finger at him as I scream, still unable to look at him. "How could you fucking forget the day your son died? Do you even fucking care?"

"Yes!" He yells back, and my head jerks back because in all the time I've known Dominick, he's never raised his voice to me. "I just can't fucking think about it all the time. I can't handle it, because if I did, I'd... I'd turn into you!" Tears spring to my eyes as he stalks toward me, and I step back at his every advance. "Look at you! This is what happens when all you do is wallow in it and do nothing else but think about it. You're miserable and you're making me miserable, for fuck's sake!"

As he steps inside, I run into the kitchen and grab a steak knife. I don't know why, but suddenly I feel unsafe. How dare he raise his voice to me!

Standing at the counter, the knife in my right hand as he enters, I hear him suck in a breath before saying in a very low, gentle tone, "Evie. Put the knife away. I'm sorry for yelling at you."

"Don't." I laugh, holding the knife with the pointy end up as I run the other end in a line, back and forth, across the granite of the countertop. Neither of us speak for several moments until I work up the courage to tell him why I brought him here. "Dominick... I want a divorce."

"What?" He walks toward me, seeming to find me holding a knife harmless, and really, why would he think I would harm him? "Evie, don't say that. I love you. We can get..." He swallows as he stops right next to me, and I wonder if he's eyeing the knife, but I refuse to look at him to even see what's on his face. I can't stand his face, because I know if I look at it, all I'll see is my baby. My sweet baby. "We can go to therapy together, Evie. Please..."

"I want a divorce." The words are so hushed, I can't even tell if I said them, or if they were all in my head.

"Evie..." He puts a hand on my shoulder and does exactly what I told him not to. "I miss Zander, too."

Anger thrums through me and for the first time in a year, I lift my gaze and look into Dominick's face as I hiss, "I said I want a fucking divorce!"

Then, I lift the knife, twist my wrist so the pointy end is down, and plunge it into the front of his shoulder under the collarbone.

And when his mouth drops open and he is no longer touching me, I take off running out to the car, and minutes later, I'm screaming as the car goes airborne.

CHAPTER 12

WHEN DOMINICK PUTS HIS HAND ON MY SHOULDER AS he sits on the bed next to me, I pretend I'm still sleeping, even though I know he'll realize quick that I'm awake.

I can't believe I stabbed him.

I drove us to the cabin in a rental car I secured with a fake name — okay, I really don't know how or why that was necessary, or how I managed it — and I stabbed him, then ran.

"I'm a terrible person," I mutter, forgetting I'm feigning sleep.

To my surprise, he chuckles. "The part of me you stabbed may beg to differ, but I don't agree."

"How can you find this amusing?" I cover my head with the pillow, groaning, and his hand squeezes my shoulder in that comforting way of his. "Dominick..."

He pulls the pillow away from my head, and with a firm, gentle hold, rolls me over on to my back.

My gaze automatically falls to his lips as old habits kick in, and I'm unable to meet his gaze.

"You didn't mean it," he says, and I watch his lips curve up as his voice fills with amusement. "And honestly, I kinda deserved it. What kind of dumbass gets close to a hysterical woman holding a knife?"

A bubble of laughter, my first real one in over a year, escapes and my hands fly up to cover my mouth as it mingles with a sob of grief at hurting the one and only person who has ever made me feel anything.

"Evie... look at me, sweetheart." He places two fingers under my chin and lifts it, but I hold my gaze down even as he begs. "Please. I know it hurts, but... you have to. It's one hurdle in a long line of hurdles, but at least look at me."

He's right, and I know he's right.

By sheer force of will, I move my eyes up from his lips, to his nose, and when I finally reach his gorgeous and gloriously alive eyes, I slam mine shut at the pain invading my body.

"It hurts. Your eyes..."

"I know, but his eyes were way better than mine. I have the dull, boring ones." My eyes snap open at this and I scowl, only to find him smiling at me as I look right into his eyes. "There. Much better."

Even as I tremble with the need to glance away, for a

few moments, I do as he bids, everything I wish to say sticking in my throat. I'm not sure I could speak even if I wanted to, and in the end, he's the one who looks down and to the side.

Taking my hand in his, he lifts it up to his lips and presses a kiss on them, and I let out the breath I didn't know I've been holding.

"I would like to take you home now."

"I—I'm not sure..."

He grips my hand tighter, cutting me off with a clearing of his throat. "Yes. I know... I know you wanted a divorce, and maybe you still do." Now it's he who won't meet my gaze with his. "But, his second birthday would be in a month and I want you to give me that. At least come home and give me a month. And if the day after, if still want it to be over..." He takes in a deep breath, and then brings his gaze back to mine. "Then, I'll do whatever you want."

I know many things right now.

I know I married a good man — no, a great man — and I know he's been here every day, even though I did not understand who he was. He's talked to me, comforted me, and held me when I cried. He loves me, and he doesn't want to lose me.

And all that is great and wonderful and I know I'm so lucky to have him; so lucky he loves me.

What I don't know, however, is how I feel or what I

want, which means my answer is one thing and one thing only.

"All right," I agree with a whisper. "Until the day after, then."

He grins then, the worry eases in his gorgeous face as he pulls me into his arms. For the first time in over a year and two months, we hug each other; as the parents of Zander, as two grief-stricken parents who've lost their child, and finally, as man and wife.

And the feel of his arms around me after so long, sweet in their hold as he cradles me like I'm the most precious thing in the world to him, is enough to begin melting the ice that's been wrapped around my heart for so long.

CHAPTER 13

Waking up in bed with your husband's leg and arm tossed over you is a weird sensation after three months in a solitary psych ward bed.

I lie here, unsure of what to do, and can't help but note the new ache in my chest.

Or should I say an old ache awakened? An ache I didn't feel when I forgot everything, and part of me wishes I were still in that state, even though I know I shouldn't desire such a thing.

Sighing, I turn my head to the side and my eyes land on a shoulder connected to the arm across my chest.

His left arm.

And on it, the damning evidence of my attack in the form of a scar. I lift my hand and rub the pad of my thumb across the mark, caressing it as if in apology, and resisting the urge to place my lips on it.

Kissing is what started this whole thing, after all.

"It didn't do any permanent damage," come the soft words from Dominick, and I move my gaze until it finds his lips turned up as he watches me in the soft morning light. Not expecting him to catch me, I flush and remove my touch. He chuckles, adjusting his body until he's hovering over and surrounding me. "It's been a long time since you were in my bed."

He's naked, and I'm the one wearing a tank and loose yoga pants, but out of the both of us, I feel like the nude one with the way he's looking at me. As if he can see through my clothing; through me.

I suppose he always has. He's always known me better than I know myself.

"Yeah." I don't rip my gaze from his, even though I long to do so, as the soft words tumble from my lips, my body responding to his proximity with a feverish awakening I haven't felt in over a year. "It has."

Dominick comes down on his elbows, supporting his weight while simultaneously making our bodies touch one another. His face is right above mine, and with a little adjustment, he's able to use his right hand to run his fingers down the side of my face until his thumb and forefinger grip my chin.

"Don't," I whisper as he leans in, and he pauses right before our lips are to touch, but doesn't move away. "I..." As I lick my lips, his grip tightens a little, eliciting a small whimper from me. "I want you to touch me... but I can't... no kissing. Not when I'm not sure..."

"It's not that you can't. It's that you won't." In one smooth movement, he rolls off me, and sits on the edge of the bed facing away from me, running a frustrated hand through his hair. "I love you, Evie. I came to see you every day, even though you wouldn't even look at me, and I waited. If I wanted a fuck without the emotions, I could've done it without you being any the wiser." He twists his body to look back at me, and frowns. "I'm not willing to sleep with you until you're giving me your all. We both deserve that and nothing less."

As he stands up, heading toward the bathroom, I don't even argue.

Because what he wants is exactly the crux of the problem.

I'm not sure I even have an all to give, especially not since the day our son died.

All the wishing in the world, all the desire to connect with the man I love, and all the tears I've shed because of how it's messing up my life mean nothing in the shadow of this grief I can't seem to shake.

And going from feeling nothing, to meeting Dominick and feeling everything, it's now as if I feel everything and nothing at the same time. It's enough to make me want to scream, but I refrain, especially when he comes back into the room and dresses.

"You should get ready," he says in his even, good-natured tone. "We have an appointment with the therapist at nine."

What? This is the first I've heard of this.

"Therapist?"

He turns around as he shrugs on his button down now that he's got his pants on and quirks a brow. "You didn't think you'd come home, and we'd do nothing except live together for a month, did you? We've got bigger problems together than either of us can solve."

"I thought nothing." My tone is defensive in an instant, but even as his lips thin at my tone, he says nothing. "W-where are my things?"

He nods at the dresser where my clothing has always been, finishing his cuffs and heading toward the door, tossing over his shoulder. "Try not to take too long, Evie. I have to make sure you eat and take your meds. And don't worry," he says with a chuckle, "I've locked up the knives."

Ah yes, my meds.

I've been on an anti-depressant and a mood stabilizer since arriving in the hospital, and while they help a little, no pill in the world can take away the sorrow which has buried itself deep inside my heart.

With a heavy sigh, I slip out of bed and over to the dresser to change, then head downstairs to start what I feel will probably be the longest month of my life.

THE VERY FIRST TIME WE MEET, WE WALK RIGHT INTO each other.

Literally.

"Oomph."

The supplies in my hands fall to the ground, scattering all over the place, and a male voice has me lifting my gaze from the ground up into his face.

Okay, well, I suppose I'm the one who walked into him, but he doesn't seem bothered.

"My apologies," he says with a wide grin. "Let me help you pick those up."

I'm stunned into silence as he bends down in front of me and starts gathering my things while all I can do is stare. He's at least six inches taller than my five-foot-five frame, with short, closely cropped brown hair, and dark eyes. I'm ashamed to admit it, but he's the most gorgeous man I've ever seen.

And okay, I guess I'm a little sheltered, and although I'm twenty now, I moved away from home for college two years ago, knowing very little about the real world. With a mother who thought the entire world was out to get her and her child, I never got to go anywhere or do anything, and she homeschooled me. So all the hot guys I saw until college were on TV and compared to the ones I've met... yep, he takes the cake.

Even though I live in the dorms, nobody ever talks to me, and when I try to talk to them, it seems they all look at me and then decide I'm not worth the effort. After my first semester, I gave up, and have been grateful for the emotional fortitude that makes me not give a shit. I'm in school to learn, not to mess around, especially if I want to have a good life. I've no desire to return home ever again.

"Are you all right?"

I jump as I realize he's speaking to me and all I'm doing is staring at him, then flush to the roots of my hair. My red hair. Which means when I flush, I look like a damn strawberry, but without the hull on top to make it official.

"Uh, yeah." He holds out the paper, pens, and book I was carrying, waiting for me to take them, which I do. "S-sorry I ran into you."

He shrugs. "No need to be sorry." Sliding one hand

into his pocket, he extends the other toward me. "I'm Dominick. And you are?"

Switching the stuff to one hand and cradling it against my body, I rub my hand on my skirt before clasping his. "Um. Constance. But I go by Evie, which is my middle name. But you can call me whatever you want."

When he laughs at my babbling, my blush deepens, and I go back to clutching my stuff against my chest with both hands.

"Nice to meet you, Evie."

"Uh, yeah. Y-you too, Dominick."

It's an odd feeling. I am nervous, and yet intrigued, too. Usually, I am oblivious to others around me, but he makes me want to stand here and chat even though I really need to get going.

This is the longest conversation I've had with someone since arriving at school, and I don't want it to end.

"You want to go out sometime?"

My mouth drops open, and even though I recover quick and snap it shut, I smile despite the bottom of my stomach dropping out in utter shock that he'd want to go out with me. "You just met me."

"Yes. And I've decided I would like to go out on a date with the girl standing in front of me blushing like she's naked." Chuckling, because his words have me turning red once more, he holds out his hand. "Give me your phone and I'll put my number in it for you."

With a deep breath, I do as he asks, and watch as he types his information in my phone.

Once he hands it back to me, I put in my pocket and he steps close, lifting a hand to my hair and pushing some stray hair behind my hair. "When you decide you want to go out, call me. And your hair is gorgeous."

"Thank you."

In a moment of curiosity, and because he's so close to me, my eyes drop from his eyes down to his lips, which curve up as I do so. I immediately move my eyes back up to his, finding them filled with amusement as his small smile turns right back into a full on grin.

Then, after a few more seconds of us staring at each other like two teenagers in love, he steps back and winks at me. "Catch you later, Evie. And remember, there is zero chance of rejection, so take a chance."

Words escape me, so all I can do is nod as he walks past me, and I take a deep breath.

As I head back to class, I have one thought.

Once I get up the nerve, I will call him, and I know Dominick will be my first kiss.

Something tells me he's the perfect man for a first kiss.

And when I take a seat in my first class of the day, I'm the happiest I've been since the day I left home.

CHAPTER 15

I DIDN'T REALLY ENJOY THERAPY IN THE PSYCH WARD — probably why I replaced sessions with my doctor with my husband in my mind — and I certainly am not enjoying marital counseling.

Five minutes or five hours, our marriage isn't the problem.

I am.

"She won't talk to me. She won't talk to anyone."

Turning my gaze from the window to Dominick, and then the therapist, I sigh. "Talking doesn't seem to help, so I don't waste my breath."

I swear, the lady gives me an empathetic smile, before dropping her gaze and writing something on the pad in her lap.

She says something, but honestly, I'm not listening anymore. I'm back to staring out the window, and they chat between themselves for a few minutes until Dominick puts his hand on my leg, making me jump.

When my eyes meet his, he says, "I need you to talk to me. I need you to tell me how you feel."

Annoyed with it all and frustrated with having to deal with this when all I want to do is crawl into a ball and cry — something my medication makes hard to achieve because it's a damn anti-depressant and I feel like it's suffocating my emotional capacity — I shrug. "Fine. I'll tell you how I feel."

I swat his hand away, standing up to go stand by the window, and without looking at either of them, I give them what they want.

"Even before I met Dominick, I had a limited range of emotions. I was in a bad mood, or a neutral mood, and mostly, I kept my emotions in check because in my mother's house, any display of them was unwanted."

I look at the therapist. "You want to know why I have difficulty sharing? That's why." I don't even glance at my husband before returning my focus out the window. I'm not even looking at anything; I just don't want to look at him. "Then, I met him, and he made me feel... well, he made me feel everything."

I lift my shoulders in a shrug, dropping them after a moment, and I know he's listening real close now. "I didn't know what it was. I figured, this must be what it's like to fall in love. I'd never been in love, never been kissed, never had a relationship until him. We were friends for a year first, and on my twenty-first birthday, he asked me to marry him. It's like the whole time we were friends, we were dating, and I didn't even know. He hadn't even kissed me yet."

I hear him chuckle behind me, and I want to smile, but like most things, it's locked up and frozen somewhere inside me.

"Of course, I said yes even though he surprised me, and we got so drunk — which being my first time drinking, it didn't take long. When I woke up the next morning, I had his ring on my finger, and he was in bed next to me, and I was wrapped in his arms. And right there, that's when he kissed me. When I had terrible hair, not so great breath, and my make-up smudged; he opened his eyes, smiled at me, and whispered, 'good morning' seconds before his lips covered mine. And I felt lucky... so, so lucky."

I pause, hugging myself closer, and look back for a brief instant at Dominick, who is watching me with an intent stare full of every emotion I wish I could feel. I turn away and continue.

"A year into our engagement, we discover I'm two months pregnant," I laugh and throw my hands up in the air for a second before lowering them, "which Dominick pointed out because I totally had no idea, as I was oblivious to my body, along with having zero signs... not even nausea. And then, a month later, we got married. I'd never been so happy in my life, and everything was going so great. So fucking great. Our son was born, and we were so happy at first. But something was wrong... something was wrong with me."

"Evie..."

I hold up a hand to stop Dominick. "I felt so disconnected from Zander. I loved him, but I felt hollow. I said nothing, though, and I tried so hard to pretend everything was okay. I figured maybe it was just me. Maybe it would get better, but the months went by and I was fucking frustrated, and tired, and overwhelmed.

He was a baby, and I got so mad. I'd put him in his crib, and he'd cry and cry, but I had to walk away. Then, I would calm down, and go back, and he'd look up at me with his beautiful little eyes and face, and simply hold up his hands, opening and closing them, saying, 'mama, mama.' I knew he deserved a mother better than me, but I picked him up and told him, 'I'm what you get, kid. I'm your mom. I hope you're okay with that.' And he would smile at me, saying, 'mama' repeatedly, clapping his hands."

A tear slips down my cheek, and I swipe at it angrily. "The day he died... I knew it was punishment for the way I treated him, for the way I couldn't be the mom he needed; couldn't feel the way he needed me to."

I whirl back around to find my husband with swollen, red eyes, and give him a sad smile. "You want to know how

I feel? I died with him that day, even more so than I was already dead on the inside my whole life. And you kept going on with yours as if nothing had changed. Rationally, I know you dealt with it the way you had to, but you do not understand how I feel and I don't deal with things the way you do. I never will."

I look at the therapist who is watching me, too, and then pick up my purse. "No amount of therapy will bring my son back, and no amount of therapy will make his death feel less like a punishment. I'm done here."

I'm out of the room before Dominick can even stand up.

I wait in the car until he comes out.

Let's just say the drive home is the loudest fucking silence I've ever experienced, and I deserve it.

CHAPTER 16

THE SILENCE PERSISTED ALL DAY YESTERDAY, BUT EVEN though I tried to sleep elsewhere, the only time Dominick spoke was to insist we would share the same bed.

So we did, because I was too damned tired to argue.

Now it's close to time for him to return home from work, and I've spent most of my day online looking for jobs.

A month before we found out I was pregnant, I graduated from college with a BS in Accounting. However, I never put it to good use because Dominick and I got married, moved in together, and soon after, I gave birth to Zander.

I hadn't minded, really. Until his birth, and even after, Dominick told me whatever I wanted to do — whether stay home or work — it was up to me, and he would support whatever decision I made. Obviously, I stayed home with

Zander. Dominick, who is five years older than me, was already established in his career as a financial advisor — one thing we'd bonded over — and owned a home, along with being financially secure. It had been the perfect arrangement, in retrospect.

But now, I need a job, because before I went job searching, I looked up lots of information on grief, and one of the many ways it says people cope is having a purpose.

And since my purpose is no longer being a mother, along with the wife part being up in the air, I think having something else to do besides sit around this house is a great idea.

Lucky for me the place where I had an internship during my coursework is looking for someone with my degree, and since I know the boss, I'm hoping both facts are enough to get me in the door.

I pick up the phone and dial the number. Once the receptionist picks up, I put on my professional voice I spent years perfecting during school, and bluff my way into being put through to the boss.

"Quinton Knight."

"Mr. Knight, this is Constance Waterbrook, although you knew me as Evie Newman..."

"Wow, Evie. It's been a while. How're you doing?"

I thought about how to answer the question. The internship had been during my last semester, so they'd all known of my engagement, and even had a small get together to say goodbye, especially since they offered me a job and I had turned it down. And although I'd considered myself friends with them, including Mr. Knight, I keep my reply professional.

"I'm doing well, and yourself?"

"Same old," he says with a chuckle, and I hear him fumbling around for a moment before he asks, "What can I do for you, Evie?"

"Well," I bite my lip, nervous at this blatant approach, but suck it up and smile, hoping the positivity conveys in my voice. "I see you have a position open — the same one you offered me years ago — and I'm hoping the offer still stands."

"I told you we'd welcome you here in the future, didn't I?"

Even though I don't remember him telling me that, I laugh and act as if I recall such a thing. "Yes, you did. And I would love to work for your firm again. I enjoyed my time there during my internship."

"Glad to hear."

After a few more minutes, and an invitation to come into the office tomorrow at one, we both hang up.

Turning off the computer and getting up, I pick up my phone and open my book reading app, aiming to relax a little. It doesn't last long, because all I've downloaded are romance books, and probably because of how I feel, I'm just disgusted with the whole idea of happily ever after.

They are a good escape, but I'm not feeling the whole 'love will conquer all' thing going on, especially since I don't feel like Dominick's love will conquer the issues I'm having.

I head to the kitchen, and moments after I enter, I hear the front door open and shut. When he comes into the kitchen, I've got the fridge door ajar, searching inside for something to eat, and he clears his throat. Taking a deep breath, I step back and close it, then turn to him with a smile.

"Okay," he says in an instant, although there's no heat in his words. "You're smiling, so that makes me suspicious."

I'm not interested in bantering, so I just come out and say what I need to say. "I have a job interview tomorrow."

"Really?" His eyebrows shoot up. "Where?"

"Remember the firm I interned at? Well, they are hiring, so I called up Mr. Knight and asked if he'd consider hiring me. He told me to come in for an interview."

"That's great, Evie." His grin exhibits his genuine happiness for me. "I think having something to do will be a great thing for you."

"Yes. I think so, too. And you won't have to deal with me moping around here all the time."

He steps closer, until we're inches apart, and cradles my face in his hands. "Your happiness is what I want. I don't like to see you mope because your sadness makes me unhappy. I feel..." He lets out a heavy breath and leans his forehead against mine. "I feel helpless, unable to do anything for you, Evie. I'm lonely, sweetheart, without you."

I wish I could say I reciprocated the way he feels, but I don't.

I'm not lonely, I'm empty. And it's not a spot he can fill in, no matter how much I wish it were so.

And it's this moment which makes it crystal clear a month together would be a waste of time and hurt him even more by the end.

The right thing to do is end it now. He deserves a fight I can't give him. Not now, and maybe never.

I shake my head, stepping back from his touch, and say, "If I get this job, Dominick, I think the best thing for me would be to move out and get a place of my own."

At my announcement, I expect a lot of things. For him to say no, I agreed to stay, or for him to persuade me to change my mind and just give it a little. But he doesn't.

His lips compress as he nods, sliding his hands into his pockets, his eyes flaring with all the emotions I know he's suppressing for my sake.

"Thank you," I whisper, my eyes filling with tears. "I wish..."

"Don't, sweetheart. I knew this was coming yesterday at the therapist's office. I did not understand how you felt about it all and I've no right to make you stay, no matter how much you leaving will hurt."

I choke up, knowing how much I don't deserve this

man and his love for me, and he steps forward to pull me into his arms. "I—I'm sorry. I j-just don't want you to h-hate me. I h-hate myself enough."

"Never."

It's all he says, but it's enough. Dominick is a man of his word, and I believe him. It doesn't make me hate myself any less, though, and as he hugs me tight, I know I don't want to leave things this way.

I don't want to say goodbye with tears.

So without a word, I lift my head and slide my hands up and around his neck, raising up on my tiptoes and kissing him square on his lips before he can gather what I'm doing.

CHAPTER 17

It's one of those moments I may look back on and wonder what the hell I was thinking, but I don't care at this point.

I want his touch; he wants to touch me, and in this moment, I'm giving him my all.

Sure those fit his criteria, he confirms it as his arms tighten around me, one hand sliding up and into my hair. He's not in a rush, though, and neither am I. At first, the kisses are soft; the kind where you're first exploring someone's lips, and your mouths barely open, but it's enough where you tease, nip, and suck in a playful, hot dance.

His other hand slips down and grips my ass, followed by him saying against my lips, "Wrap your legs around me."

I do as he bids, jumping to wrap my legs as I cling to

him, and our mouths never leave one another as he carries me up the steps. We finally break apart as I fall back on the bed, and he unbuttons his shirt enough to pull it over his head. I undress, and within minutes, I'm scooting up the bed as he climbs on. When my head hits the pillow, I lie back as he sits by my feet and takes them in his hands, caressing the soles with the pad of his thumb.

And then, as we both stare at the other, he grins. "I know I never told you this, but us meeting as we did was no accident."

"What?"

He brings his hands over to slide up my left leg, spreading them to glide over my hips, then plants them at my sides as he covers my body with his. When he looks down into my face, it's with an expression of extreme seriousness.

"I told you my visit was to a professor friend on campus that day, and it was, but you and I didn't bump into each other because both of us weren't watching where we were going. You were walking toward me, and I thought you were the prettiest woman I'd ever lain eyes on." He lifts a hand and pushes my hair behind my ear, leaning in and giving me a sweet, tender kiss. "I veered right into your path so I would have the opportunity to introduce myself, and it worked."

I believe it, but I'm still taken aback. "Dominick..."

He places a finger over my mouth and shakes his head.

"I was attracted to you the moment I saw you, and since then, it hasn't dissipated. You gave birth to my child, you're the most beautiful woman to me even now, and I don't see my opinion ever changing there."

He pauses and looks away, and I watch him struggle to keep his feelings under control in a way I've never had to before. He pinches the bridge of his nose, and keeps his face averted as he speaks, voice raw with his emotions. "You blamed me when he died, and maybe you should. After everything that's happened, sometimes I wonder if what I did that day to make sure we met wasn't selfish of me. I think maybe you weren't meant for me, and our son wasn't meant to be born, and that's why..."

He sucks in a breath and releases it in a shuddering exhalation as my eyes tear up, but when his eyes return to mine, they are filled with fire. "Maybe it's true, and maybe it's not, but I don't regret one fucking minute of it. And perhaps it's selfish of me to tell you this now, but I thought you should know it was on purpose. I chose you, Evie, and I've loved you the best way I know how. I know it's not good enough, and I know you'll get this job, and you'll leave. And that's okay, because all I want is your happiness, even if it doesn't include me. Even if it hurts like hell because I know there's nothing I can do to keep it from happening."

Tears trickle down my cheeks, his confession leaving me speechless, but in the end that doesn't matter. He takes his comfort from me, capturing my lips and seeking immediate entrance, and at the same time, his touch gives me solace. His weight comes down on me as he shoves both hands into my hair, taking and taking from my mouth as I wrap my legs around him. With the practice and knowledge of a man who knows my body and his body all too well, he thrusts his cock inside me in one fluid stroke, and we both gasp in the other's mouth simultaneously.

I might be telling myself this to make us breaking up better, but something in this moment — the one where we come together even as we fall apart — is so beautiful. And I may feel this way because we aren't angry, we aren't bitter, and it's not a fight. We've accepted the inevitable end of us for now, maybe even forever, yet there is love between us.

We'll always love the time we spent together, and we'll always love the son we shared for his brief life, and yes, we'll even love each other even if it's not the love which, according to so many, should sustain us through all this pain and more. Because the beauty of love is knowing, with every part of you, that this person is the one for you. The ugliness is learning that sometimes, not even love is enough to overcome everything shoving its way in between, and any crack, any weakness, may bring it all tumbling around you when you're not well enough to fight back.

I went into this marriage believing loving him would mean we'd last forever, but that was my naiveté; my inexperience with the real world, and all the damage it could deliver to my life when I least expected it.

Dominick moves in and out at a slow and steady pace, drawing this time with us out, his left hand tightening on my hair and baring my neck as the other slides down. He rests it on my neck, his thumb resting on the pulse there for a few seconds, before he slips his hand down to my chest and places his palm against the beat of my heart.

Connected with our mouths fused, our bodies loving each other, and his hand over my heart, he shows me his love and understanding. And I show him mine, along with how sorry I am that I can no longer be the woman he married, and when it's over... when we're both crying our silent tears, which stream down our cheeks without so much as a sniffle between us, he cradles me to him and I let him hold me.

Because in the morning we'll wake up and nothing will ever be the same.

But for tonight I'll pretend I'm not saying goodbye, and he'll pretend this isn't the last time he'll ever make love with his wife.

CHAPTER 18

THE TENSION THAT'S HAUNTED ME AND DOMINICK since our son's death is gone the next morning. For once, I feel as if I can breathe around him. He gets up and walks over to the dresser to get ready for work as usual, but even in the silence, there is no awkwardness.

When he's finished dressing, he turns around and comes back over to the bed, leans over, and kisses me on the cheek. "I'm sure you have the job just by calling, but all the same, good luck."

"Thank you." I sit up as he steps back and grabbing his hand, I squeeze it while smiling up at him. "I'm sure I have it, too."

His lips curve up as he lifts my hand to his mouth and presses a kiss to the back of it. "Have a good day."

Then he walks over to his side of the bed, grabs his things, and heads out.

I lie back and wonder what I should wear, and whether I have anything that will fit, anyway. I'm not as skinny as I had been before Zander was born, so I may need to go shopping before the interview.

Sliding out of bed and hopping in to get a quick shower, a quick perusal of my wardrobe confirms the fact I will need something new and updated to wear. Sliding on a pair of loose flowing pants and a tank, I brush out my hair before twirling it into a bun and securing it on my head. Soon, I'm on my way to the shopping center, looking forward to purchasing something for myself for the first time in a long while.

I used to truly enjoy going to the store. Even before Dominick and I married, he would take me shopping and buy me everything I needed even if I didn't want him to, and I always objected, but he insisted. I gave in, of course, because I wanted to make him happy.

As I look through the dress casual section, I can't help but reflect on what he admitted last night.

He had taken me by surprised, but I'm not shocked by learning he set us up to meet that way. He is, and always has been, the guy who goes after what he wants, and he does it so charmingly you never realize he's getting his way. When you finally do, everything is going great, and you're wondering why you were resisting in the first place.

Well, I never resisted him, in any way, shape, or form.

I made it easy for him, and he got what he wanted; we both got what we wanted.

And perhaps ended up with what we deserved. But that's my guilt talking, and I know it.

Problem is, even when you know something in your head is wrong, it's still hard to get rid of the way you believe about something. I suspect I don't know how to let it go because I've never felt this way.

I don't know if it's even appropriate to let it go. I can't shake the feeling of how letting it go will mean I'll forget about my son. Rationally, I know it's not true; my son will always be with me in my head and heart. But it doesn't stop me from thinking it all the same.

All this leads to me knowing I need to tell Dominick I don't blame him. It's not right to blame him, and our son didn't die because he maybe should've not existed in the first place. That's ridiculous.

Both of are just too close to it and can't see the real purpose of his life and death, and probably never will because it's so personal.

I don't know.

With a sigh, I take what I've decided on — a few skirts, some blouses, and a matching jacket for all the skirts — and take it to the check out, which doesn't take long. And once I return home, I dress, do my hair along with putting on some light makeup, and sit at my desk, waiting.

And waiting.

See, the big problem is I have nothing to do, nowhere to go, and nobody to spend time with.

I've never made friends, before and even after I met Dominick, other than the people he knew. And even when you are with someone, the friends are really always the friends of the person you married, even if they let you join in. Not to mention, they were mostly unmarried men, and Dominick spent less time with them once we wed because he didn't go out and do everything with them all the time. One or two of them might've gotten married since, but I can't say I've been paying attention.

Now, working will give me something to do and somewhere to go; perhaps, too, it will finally get me a friend or two. Or, at the very least, a friend to spend time with so when I have a new place, I won't feel so damn lonely.

So, to pass time until I need to leave, I surf the internet, laugh at a few random videos, and before long it's time to go.

On my way out, I stop in front of the mirror in the hallway to make sure my make-up and hair is all neat and tidy, and as I go to fix a few stray pieces of hair which have gotten loose, my wedding ring twinkles when the light from the window lands on it just right.

I stare at the ring, this symbol of love, hope, and devotion, and when taking it off doesn't bother me as I know it should, I know I've made the right decision.

As I place the ring in a little bowl on the table, I give into the need to whisper, "I'm sorry."

And, for a moment, I keep my eyes on the ring, feeling defeated.

Then, standing up straight and squaring my shoulders, I grab my purse and head out the door to the place I hope will help me start a new life, and give me a new, desperately needed purpose.

CHAPTER 19

Sitting and waiting for my first ever actual job interview is nerve-wracking.

And exciting.

I haven't been waiting long, and I straighten up as the receptionist returns to her desk, smiling at me.

"Mr. Knight will see you now." She nods at the door to my right.

"Thank you." Standing, I smooth my skirt, take a deep breath, and stand up straight as I walk to the door and open it.

Once I've stepped inside and shut the door behind me, he turns around in his chair and smiles. "Evie. Good to see you. Come in and take a seat." He waves at a chair before picking up his water bottle and taking a drink.

Returning his smile with one of my own, I take a seat

in the indicated chair and try to sit up straight as possible. "Thank you, Mr. Knight."

"Quinton, please," he insists as he sets the water bottle back down on his desk. "I've never been big on being called Mr. Knight, as you know. Reminds me too much of my father. Great man that he was, he was also formidable and scary."

I laugh, remembering the stories he used to tell me about his father, and nod. "All right, Quinton then."

He winks at me. "You err on the side of caution, which is always a wise choice, especially when dealing with clients." He interlaces his fingers, leaning forward on his desk, his light blue eyes shining. "How've you been, Evie? Truly."

Staring at Quinton, I'm not sure how much I should share. Sure, three years ago everybody had been relaxed, and the atmosphere was one of friendliness and joviality. Always serious with clients, but when nobody was around, it became a bunch of twenty and thirty-something's playing pranks on one another and having a good time. It had been one of the few places where I felt I fit in, even though I'd only had one semester of internship.

"I'm all right." I shrug and sit back, relaxing. "Everything could always be worse."

He nods, grimacing when the phone rings, and holds up a finger. "Excuse me for just a second."

While he rambles on the phone — I don't pay attention

to what he's saying — I study Quinton. At the time of my internship, he'd only been the boss for two years, having taken over for his father once he'd fallen ill. Quinton had only been twenty-six — which made him thirty-one now since he turned twenty-eight while I interned here — and everyone tried to treat him as if he were his father, but he'd made it very clear they were nothing alike.

Physically, he has changed little. If I remember right, he's about five-eleven, and although he's skinnier than Dominick, he looks as in shape as he'd always been. His hair is dark blonde with lighter streaks; we used to tease him about them, but he always insisted they were natural and brought out more by sunlight. Either way, he's a good looking man, and last I knew, he wasn't dating anyone. A quick glance at his ring finger shows he either isn't married or engaged, or doesn't bother with a ring.

Which makes me go to fiddle with mine, only to remember I've taken it off.

Dammit. That will take some getting used to.

He hangs up the phone and puts his focus back on me. "Sorry about that. Now, where were we?"

"You were being nosy about how I am."

"Right." He coughs and laughs a little. "I'm sorry. I heard through the grapevine about your son..."

"Ah. I should've figured."

"My receptionist, once I told her you'd be coming in today, informed me of it. She's apparently the friend of the wife of one of your husband's former friends." At the quirk of my brow, he rushes to assure me, "Don't worry. I told her she isn't to say anything to you or anyone else, as it's your business. But, I'm sorry for your loss, and anything you need..."

I tear up, unable to help myself, and after a few moments where I work hard at pushing the tears back inside, I nod. "I appreciate it." Then I clear my throat and smile. "I'm looking forward to working with you. It'll be nice to..." I wave my hand with a laugh. "Well, it'll be nice to do something productive."

"Absolutely."

He goes into the spiel about what I'll be doing, my salary, and all that; all details I knew from the job listing itself. Once he's done, he hands me some papers to fill out and sits back. I stare down at the paperwork, my mouth going dry as I struggle with what to put for the simplest question.

My name.

"Quinton?"

He leans forward, instantly alert. "Problem?"

"Um..." I swallow and twiddle with the pen, then give him an 'I feel stupid' half-smile because I can't tell him I feel awkward as hell asking something I should know the answer to. "Is it all right if I put my maiden name in? It's not official yet, but..."

"Oh." He says as my word trail off, his eyes drop to my

left hand, and the obvious line where my ring used to be, then nods. "Sure, sure, if that's how you'll be filing your taxes."

It's silent as I finish filling the papers out, handing them over to him once I'm done, and grabbing my purse. "When shall I start?"

"How about tomorrow? I must go out of town for a few days the day after, so at least you'll have me here for your first day in case you need anything."

"Great." I stand up, and when he holds out his hand, I shake it. "I'll see you then."

I've almost reached the door when I turn back around and find him watching me, as I ask, "Quinton, do you know where some good places to live are? I'm getting an apartment, but I know little about this area, really. I'd like to live close to here."

"Yes, I do. I'll bring in a list for you tomorrow, if you'd like."

"Thanks."

"Anything you need, Evie," he reassures me in a kind voice. "I mean it."

"Right."

With that, I turn and head out the door to return home and start packing my things.

CHAPTER 20

My first day of work is uneventful, yet being around other people makes me feel happier than I have in a long time.

And as the end of the day rolls around, Quinton approaches with what seems his permanent don't-give-a-shit grin on his face. "Evie. How'd your first day go?"

"Great," I say with an answering smile. "Everyone is so nice. Yours?"

"I fielded phone calls all day. Always exciting." He extends a hand to include the others as they get ready to go. "We're going out for drinks. Want to come?"

"Really?"

"Yes," he says with an eye roll and takes my hand, tugging me up and leaving me with barely enough time to grab my purse before we're heading across the room.

"Everyone, Evie is coming. She'll be a lush right along with us before long!"

They all laugh, and I join in with a nervous chuckle of my own.

We exit, Quinton locking up and still holding my hand, while everyone else heads to their cars.

"Ah... I'm over there." I point to my car as he starts walking before stopping abruptly.

"I can drive and bring you back to your car later, if you want," he says with a quirk of his brow. "We can talk about those apartments you were interested in on the way since I forgot the paper."

I look at my car, then at him, and shrug. "Okay. I suppose it doesn't matter either way."

"Great." He unlocks the door, holding it open for me as I slide in, then gets in the other side. "Do you need to let anyone know where you're going?"

Well, that's an odd question. "What?"

"I'm sorry," he says without looking at me, starting up the car and pulling out of the parking spot. "I assumed since you're needing a place to stay, you're still living with your husband, and might need to tell him you aren't coming home straightaway."

"No." My reply is short, and I wince as he tosses me a perplexed look. "I mean, I don't think he expects me to tell him my every move, but maybe I should send him a text, anyway."

"Okay." He shrugs. "It's not my business either way, so next time just tell me to shut it."

Unable to prevent a laugh from escaping, I chuckle as he focuses on the road, and pull out my phone to send Dominick a text. I'm not sure what I'm doing really, so better to be safe than sorry, and have Dominick freaking out because I didn't come home when I said I would on my first day.

'Going out for drinks with my co-workers, so won't be home right away.'

I receive a response as Quinton pulls into our destination and parks the car.

'All right, have fun. And thanks for telling me, you didn't have to. See you when you get home.'

Sliding the phone into my purse, I give Quinton a thumbs up as we exit the car. "All done. I think it surprised him I told him."

"Yeah well," he says as we walk inside the bar and head toward the back where the other's have already sat down. "Better to tell him just in case something happens."

Right. Well, at least he's no longer holding my hand, although I don't think he means anything by it other than being friendly. And we still haven't discussed those apartments.

The four other people I work with — two men, Garrison and Matthew, and two women, Jessica and

Lorraine — smile at us as we sit down, and before long we've ordered drinks.

"I've been waiting all day to tell you all this!" Jessica practically bounces in her seat before displaying her left hand and showing off her ring. "I'm engaged!"

Everyone congratulates her — apparently, she left her ring off until after work so she could say it while out tonight — and Quinton lifts his drink in the air. "May you... and what's his name—" We all laugh while Quinton grins and Jessica says, "Trevor" with an eye roll. "Right, right. May you and Trevor live happily forever after in wedded bliss."

Lifting our drinks, we join in the toast and take a drink, but suddenly I feel jealous at how happy she is.

Trying not to examine that too closely, I sit back and listen as they all rattle on and on about this or that in their lives. And the whole time, Quinton watches me, even as he pays attention to the surrounding conversation.

After a drink or two — which I only have one because of my meds — along with some food, they are all standing up and heading home.

And we're back in Quinton's car on the way to the office.

"So," he says softly, "there are a lot of options for apartments around here. You can stay where Jessica and Lorraine live, although I'm sure Jessica will move in with Trevor. She's been waiting forever for him to propose, so now that he's finally done it, I'm sure they'll get married before long."

I laugh at the derisive quality of his statement and when I look over, find him scowling at the road. "Never married, Quinton?"

"Hell no. I came close once though."

"What happened?"

"Dunno." He shrugs and turns the corner. "Everything was going fine, and right before I planned to propose, she broke up with me. I saw her about a year later, and she had married someone else. They were about to have a baby. I'm happy for her."

"When was this?"

He laughs. "Right before you came to intern, actually. So a while now. I haven't dated since; too much of a fucking headache."

"Maybe you should consider yourself lucky you didn't marry her. Doesn't sound like she was as invested as you were in the relationship."

"Yeah." He clears his throat as he pulls into the parking spot next to my car. "So, there are those apartments. I know my place has a few spots open they are filling. And, there are more in that area." He pulls out a card from his pocket and writes on the back of it, then hands it to me. "There's the name of a few places you should check out."

I look down at the list for a moment before putting it inside my purse. "Thanks. I'll do that this weekend."

"Hey." He puts his hand on my shoulder as I go to open the door, and I look back over at him with an expectant look. "I know it's none of my business, so you can tell me to fuck off if you want, but what happened? I remember your husband — your fiancé at the time — and he was crazy about you. And you were crazy about him."

I stare at him, worrying my lip between my teeth, trying to decide what to say. How can I answer his question when I don't even know what happened? When I'm not even sure what I felt for Dominick was real in the first place, and how sometimes I feel as if what we had was an illusion; one made up by a lonely girl who never had any friends and wanted someone to love her. Was there any way to really say this to anyone?

No, I decide, there isn't, so I go with the simplest answer.

"I don't know," I answer him with a shrug, and his hand slips off my shoulder as I choose my words carefully. "Life happened, I guess. I went from living at home, to college, to engaged, then married and having a baby. So we're getting divorced, I will get my own place, and be on my own for a while. Make some friends."

Try to feel less empty.

Yeah, not gonna go there.

And even though I'm not sure if he's interested in me or not, he takes my statement in stride, not even blinking.

"You're off to a good start, Evie. You've already got one friend, at least."

"Right." Laughing, I step out of the car, and then lean in. "Thanks for the drink, and for the job. I assume I'll see you Monday?"

"Yes, see you then."

I close the door and once I'm inside my car, he pulls away.

And I'm left shaking my head as I head home, with what feels like the first real, natural smile I've had in a long time plastered on my face.

CHAPTER 21

I walk through an apartment up for rent with Dominick by my side.

Although I insisted he didn't have to come with me, he'd been adamant about checking the places out and making sure I found somewhere "safe and secure" to live in. He also made it clear we were and always would remain friends, so I should accept his help since that's what friends do. I didn't have the heart to deny his help, especially since this was going against everything he wanted just to make me happy.

This is the third complex we've looked at, and none of them really appeal to me.

"Why don't you buy a place, Evie?" He mutters underneath his breath as the lady rattles on and on about the apartment. "I'll buy you a townhouse or something. You'll get money in the divorce, anyway."

"I don't want your money."

"And I don't want you living in a place where I will worry about you."

Smothering a laugh, I pat his hand, which rests on my arm reassuringly, and whisper, "I need to do this on my own. I'll be fine, I swear."

"I wish you'd listen to reason." The words are a grumble as he gets the lady's attention. "We'll pass. Thank you." He drags me out of the apartment and down to the car before I can even summon up a protest. "What's the next place? Hopefully it's better than the last three you've dragged me to."

"No need to be so rude, Dominick." I climb in and buckle my seat belt. "I'm sure I'll find a place."

Turning the key in the ignition, he sighs, one filled with intense aggravation. "You're being impossible. And extremely fucking stubborn."

"What?"

He smacks his hand into the wheel, making me jump, before gripping it as he glares out the windshield. "You're leaving me, Evie. I'm trying to stay patient, and be kind, because I know... fuck, I don't know what I know." He turns his gaze to me, holding his hands up in a helpless gesture. "The least you could fucking do is let me make sure you're safe. Let me help you; you've never been out on your own."

"Well, that's both our faults," I say, tearing my eyes

away from his and staring out the window. "I went from home, to a dorm, to your house. I never lived on my own, but I can't fucking learn if everyone wants to hold my damned hand like I'm a child. If I let you buy me a place to live, what does that solve?"

"Evie." He says nothing until I look back over at him, then he cups one side of my face in his hand. "We're divorcing. You'll get money because it's part yours. It's not my money; it's your money. So be smart and buy a place to live with it. It's one less thing to worry about. You can live on your own and learn all you want without struggling in the meantime."

It doesn't matter that he makes sense; it's not what I want.

"Or," I retort with a glare, "I keep the money in the bank just in case and do things on my own, like I want to do. You don't get it, and I don't expect you to, but I want to do it by myself. I need to."

He continues to stare at me, but he must see something in my face because his shoulders relax, and he starts up the car with a shrug. "All right. Where to next?"

"Silver Grove."

He whistles low, pulling out into traffic, and tosses me a smile. "Those will be on the high end of what you can afford. A nice place, though."

"Really? Well, I think in this case, it's a 'get what you

pay for' kind of thing. So far, they were all cheap — and they looked it, too."

"Yes, they were," he agrees before placing all his focus on the road.

Within a few minutes, we've arrived and after a few more, we're shown into a one-bedroom apartment on the ground-floor.

And, in an instant, I'm in love with it.

The man showing us the apartment — Peter is his name — rattles off the amenities, but I'm not listening. Heading over to the sliding doors, I open them and step out onto the patio that allows me a view of the beautiful lake in the center.

I don't even need to see the rest of the apartment. I know this is where I want to live.

I turn around to say so, stepping inside, and Dominick takes my hand in his. "I see you've already made your decision, but how about we look at the rest for the hell of it. Okay?"

Nodding, Peter shows us the rest of the apartment. It has an open floor plan, with the living room to the right of the entryway, an area by the sliding doors that can be used as a dining room, and a good-sized kitchen with a laundry room attached. Down the hall, a big bathroom with a shower-bath mix, and the master bedroom.

"I love it," I tell Peter, and he smiles at me. "How much is it?"

He names a price and my mouth drops open, while Dominick's brows rise.

"That's cheap for a place like this," Dominick says. "What's the catch?"

Peter laughs. "No catch. You say you work for Mr. Knight, which means you qualify for a lower rate, as we are involved in business with him."

"I see why he recommended this place then."

And I'm seeing why he sent me to a bunch of crap-hole places first. He knew this place would look great in comparison, and I'd be happy with the price.

I must tell him well-played when I see him.

"So you will take it then?" At my nod, Peter nods and smiles wider. "Excellent. Let's go fill out the paperwork, shall we?"

"Great."

Peter exits first, and both Dominick and I stand there for a moment knowing this is it.

"Are you sure?"

His question is soft, and I know he's not asking about the apartment, but about us. And I know he wants me to suddenly say, no, I'm not sure. And the dimming of his eyes as I stand there gazing up at him makes me wish I could tell him what he wants to hear just so his eyes will light up once more, but I can't. And he knows it.

"Yes," I reply gently. "I'm sure."

He releases my hand then, and I know for sure he's given up now.

We've ended.

And this is our new individual beginnings, whether or not he likes it.

CHAPTER 22

Today would have been Zander's second birthday.

I'm standing at his grave, and although I'm a few minutes early for when I'm supposed to meet Dominick, I'm glad for the time alone.

I bend down, slide my fingers across the lettering on his headstone, and as tears for my baby slide down my cheeks, say what I need to say.

"I'm sorry, Zander. You were my precious baby, and I know I did the best I could, but I'm still sorry. I'm sorry this is my first visit here. I didn't forget you, I swear. I just... I didn't know I was sick, but I should've gotten help. I should've realized it wasn't normal to feel the way I did, and I should've said something. You were just a baby, and I wasn't mad at you; I was mad at myself for being unable to feel how I thought I should feel."

Taking a deep shuddering breath, I take out the picture of him I carry with me everywhere — one Dominick had taken where Zander grins up at the camera, hands in mouth — and kiss it before setting it down on the headstone as I continue.

"I know people don't understand, but it's hard to let you go, and not because I imagine what you'd be like now. It's rough for me with you gone; I don't like to think about what you would be like now, because it's torture. I imagine it brings other peace, but for me, I don't like fantasies. I want to remember you as were, and you'll always be a baby to me."

A light breeze flows by, fluttering my hair, and even though the rational part of me knows it's just the wind, there's a part of me which hopes it's my son telling me he understands.

"I love you," I whisper. "And I'll always love you, no matter what happens in my life. And I miss you, with an anguish I can't describe to anyone, not even myself. And sometimes I wish I could get past the pain, and love your daddy the same as I did when we made you, but I can't. And I don't want to hurt him anymore. I want him to be happy, and I think he'll be happier with someone who isn't me. He can't see it now; maybe because we lost you and now he's losing me, but he will."

Leaves crunch as someone walks up the pathway toward me, so I swipe at my eyes while getting to my feet.

It's no surprise when Dominick steps up beside me as I straighten up, and slides his hand down until our fingers interlace with the ease of what's always been between us.

"I love that picture of him," he says, squeezing my hand and smiling at me.

"Me too."

And that's all we say.

Standing there in companionable silence for I'm not sure how long, I lean my head on his shoulder and for a crazy second, wish I would wake up from this nightmare where I've lost my son, and for a brief time, my sanity. But it's all real, and I will not wake up. This is my new reality, and all I can do is make the best of it.

"Let me walk you back to your car."

With a nod, I bend down and pick up my picture, placing it back in my purse before turning with Dominick toward the parking lot.

"How's the sale going?"

Dominick shrugs, squinting as he stares straight ahead. "About as well as it can, I suppose. I've already found a place and I've started moving."

"Have you? That's good."

After I moved out three weeks ago, Dominick informed me he would sell the house, because he felt it was too big for him and only him to live in. I agreed to the sale, but since the house is and always has been in his name, he didn't have to ask me. I appreciated the gesture, though.

He walks me over to where our cars are parked side by side, dropping me off at my driver's side door before walking over to his, and reaching inside for a brown envelope. Then, when he stops in front of me once more, he holds the envelope out to me with a grim smile, and I take it.

"You're officially Evie Newman once more."

Ah, my divorce papers. We agreed on everything and the papers, along with the separation agreement, had been drawn up a week after I moved out. Still, this was fast.

"I didn't expect it to happen so soon." My words are rueful, and rather amused, as I clutch the envelope to my chest. "Thank you."

"Two people in agreement, and a judge for a friend? You can accomplish anything."

Laughing, I open the door and drop the papers on my seat, then turn back to face him. "Dominick... you're the best."

"I know."

We stand there — him with his hands in his pockets and emotions swirling in his eyes, and me with my hands clasped in front of me, unsure of what to say in response to that — until he lifts a hand and cups my face in his hands. Leaning in, he presses a soft, sweet kiss on my lips and I wait to feel what I've always felt when he kisses me, but the electricity between us which had always shown itself when we touched is no longer there.

It's just a goodbye kiss between former lovers who are no more.

And as he pulls back, I see his acknowledgment of it in his eyes even as his lips curve up and he clears his throat, stepping back. "I'll talk to you later, all right?"

At my nod, he turns on his heel and walks around his car, tossing me one last smile before getting inside. Moments later, he turns the corner and once he's out of my sight, I slide behind the wheel of mine and head back to my place.

The place where I'll spend at least the next year being by myself; healing, making friends, working, and building a life for myself. On my own.

And maybe one day I'll date and try to have a family again.

But I'm not in a hurry.

After all, I've got my whole life ahead of me.

With a smile, I roll down the window and turn the music up, knowing when I get home I'll put the picture of Zander in the frame I picked out, and place it on my desk.

That way, every day will be a day my baby will smile at me while I work at being healthy and strong, and ready to face the world like I should've been when he was alive.

And I'll be a woman I can finally be proud of.

CHAPTER 23

"Excuse me?"

Quinton's lips curve up with his natural devil-may-care attitude, his sky-blue eyes hardening as he speaks into the phone, and sits back in his chair behind his desk.

Sitting across from him, I'm so glad the person on the other end isn't me because I know without a doubt they are about to get their ass handed to them. I've been working with Quinton for over two years now, and I've learned he's not a person you want to piss off.

It was good to discover he's human, though. His initial appearance as someone who doesn't really give two shits is nice, but it gets old quickly when he's always happy, making you wonder if he's on drugs and if so, what kind.

Of course, he's always nice to me, for obvious reasons.

One reason being he hopes to persuade me to date him and has spent the better part of the previous year attempting to make his case. So far he has gotten nowhere, and it's not for a lack of trying.

I just haven't been sure I'm ready. If I'll ever be ready.

However, I don't think me saying that will put him off for much longer.

And I'm not exactly sure why I continue denying him anymore.

"No," he bites out, leaning forward and speaking into the phone, his voice quiet and angry. "I'm paying you for your services, and if you continue to delay, I will remove you from the project and give it to someone else. You won't get paid for anything more than what you've done, contract or not. In case you've forgotten, contracts go both ways, and when you cannot deliver on your promise, it means you don't get paid, Mr. Hedge. So I advise you get your ass moving and do your job."

Mr. Hedge must have raised his voice, as I can hear his tirade if not make out his words, but Quinton doesn't seem to care as he hangs up the phone. Then, he looks down at his watch, up at the computer screen, and finally, at me.

His grin says it all. "I'm starving. Want to get some dinner?"

By now, I know this for what it is: his way of asking for a date without asking outright for one.

It's become a game between us since he asks me every day, and I always decline.

But I won't today, and it's because I don't want to be alone, which probably isn't the best time to finally say yes.

I don't expect him to remember what day it is, and I don't want to tell him because I don't want him to feel sorry for me. I want him as he is, and as he is, he'll keep me from being too sad.

He lifts a brow, waiting patiently for me to say no as usual, and I smile at him while standing up. "Sure. Why not?"

"But—" He begins, then realizes what I've said and holds up a finger, both of his brows rising in surprise. "Did you just agree? Hold on, I have to mark this down on my calendar."

I roll my eyes, unable to resist responding to his sarcasm, even if it's good-natured. "Do you want to go to dinner or not?"

In a flash, he shuts off his computer, stands up, and comes around the desk to loop his arm through mine. "Absolutely. I know the perfect place."

"I'm sure you do."

We head outside after he locks up, both of us getting into his car.

Typically when we leave work, I'll get into his car, and he'll take me home. Since we work the same hours, neither of us has seen the point in driving separately to the same place.

Of course, this came about after I discovered Quinton

lives in the same apartment complex as me, which made sense since he has business with Silver Grove and even recommended the place to me.

Now, as he pulls into traffic, he takes a left instead of the usual right and tosses a smile my way. "What made you change your mind?"

What I should say is, "Oh, it's just my deceased son's fourth birthday, and I don't want to be alone."

I don't, though. Instead, I shrug and tell him, "Perhaps I'm just famished."

"Ouch." He holds a hand up to his heart and makes an exaggerated pout face. "It hurts to know you're using me for a free dinner, Evie."

Because he looks so absurd making that face, I laugh and say, "Shut up. Why do you think I said yes?"

"I hope it's because you finally realized how hot I am and want to treat me to dinner to seduce me."

"Getting ahead of yourself there, aren't you?"

"No," he retorts with a shake of his head. "Being ahead of myself would mean I've already imagined us with a house in the country, a white picket fence, two-and-a-half kids, and a dog. And perhaps a cat."

His absurdity wrings a small giggle out of me. "Are you sure you haven't? That's horribly detailed."

He laughs, tossing me a wink before focusing on the road again.

Honestly, Quinton amuses me. For a majority of the

time, he's in a good mood; laughing and joking as if he hasn't a care in the world. And he's a good man, with a glimpse of an asshole here and there, but everyone has their limits.

I know I do.

As he pulls into a parking lot, I note the fact we're somewhere I've never been, surrounded by buildings, and there are no signs, but the sound of music is coming from close by. He parks the car, gets out and comes to my side to open my door.

"What is this place?" I ask while stepping out, where he instantly takes my hand in his, squeezing it.

"One of my favorite places to go."

We head toward a door where I see a few people enter and look up at Quinton with a raised brow. "Does it have a name?"

"Sure," he replies with a shrug as he holds the door open once we reach it, sweeping his hand toward the inside to show I should walk through. "People call it 'Hot Tots' because the owner's favorite food is tater tots."

"Really? Tater tots?"

He follows me inside without answering, and we head down a hallway toward another door, which is where the music is coming from. I stop short once we're inside, unsure how to classify this place from what I see. There is a bar, and a dance floor, with booths along the one wall, and an area with tables and chairs. Then, there is an area up above which looks closed off, and people dressed up way more than the people below.

Quinton grips my hand tighter, pulling me close to his side as a woman in a white blouse and black skirt walks toward us with a smile on her face.

"Quint," she squeals, throwing her arms around him once she reaches us and kissing him on the cheek before pulling back. "It's been ages since I've seen you here. We've missed you!"

"Clarissa, I've been busy. We'll have a table at the top, please."

She eyes me, glancing at me real quick from head to toe with a nod in greeting, then returns her hot-for-him gaze to Quinton. "You want to see Verna? She'll be real excited you're here!"

"Of course. Send her my way once you've seated us."

Clarissa nods, gathering up the menus before walking away, and we follow her.

"So you're a regular here?"

"Yeah." Quinton shrugs, his voice rising over the music. "Well, I used to come here a lot, but it's been a while."

"Since your dad died?"

He nods, saying nothing else as we head up the steps, and I feel bad. His father died shortly before I interned at the firm five years ago, so if he loves this place, then staying away must've meant they came here together.

Once Clarissa seats us and walks off to get Verna, I ask him what I see as the obvious question. "Why bring me here after all this time?"

"Easy," he says, his usual carefree smile back in place as he teases me. "I'm bringing one of my favorite people to my favorite place. Ask a harder question."

"All right." I look around the place for a moment, pondering what I should ask, and then look back at him with a mischievous grin. "Did you and Clarissa have a thing? She's hot for you, in case you didn't know."

"Good evening," a waitress says as she stops at our table before Quinton can respond. "I'm Mandy, and I'll be your server tonight. What can I get you two to drink?"

"Jack and Coke."

Quinton quirks a brow after he orders, and although I rarely drink, I join in for once. And since the doctor took me off my meds a year ago, I don't have to worry about any nasty side effects.

"I'll have an Amaretto sour, please."

She beams at us both. "Great! I'll be right back with those."

"She's awful cheerful," I say with a laugh as she walks away before lifting an expectant brow at Quinton. "Well? Did you?"

He leans back in his chair, grinning widely. "I did, but it was a while ago. We've only been friends since before I took over the firm. I don't know if she's still got a thing for me, but even if she does, I'm not interested as my sights are set elsewhere."

"You mean on me?"

The voice has us both jumping at the voice, and I look over to see the woman who must be Verna standing next to our table, hands on her hips. She's a skinny older woman — I'd say in her sixties — with short gray hair and green apple colored eyes. And her adoring eyes are focused on Quinton, who pushes back his chair with a laugh and stands up, embracing the woman with gusto.

"Verna, so good to see you. Sorry, I've not come by; I know phone calls are nothing compared to my presence."

"Oh you," she says with teary eyes, pulling back to stare up into his face. "I'll take ya anyway I can getcha. And who's this with you?"

I stand up and hold out my hand before Quinton can say something outrageous, which I know he will if he gets the chance. "Hi. I'm Evie. I work with Quinton."

When Quinton releases her, she doesn't even take my hand; instead, she pulls me into a hug, and unused to being touched, I'm too shocked to react more than with a gasp. She pulls back with an even bigger smile. "Nice to meet you. If you're a friend of Quinton's, you're a friend of mine. Y'all order yet?"

"No, we're waiting on drinks."

"Well, it's on me." She steps away and holds up a hand as Quinton opens his mouth to object. "Don't be arguing with me. Have some of my tater tots on the house; they're the best, and they're homemade."

Well, who can argue with that? "Yes, ma'am."

"Oh Lordy, girl, don't call me ma'am. I'm not that old."

"Right," I respond with a cheeky grin. "My mistake."

She nods at me, then at Quinton. "You two enjoy your dinner. I've gotta get back to the kitchen. And you," she points at Quinton, eyes growing misty again. "You better come see me more often."

"I will."

Verna walks off and up comes Mandy. She takes our order and within a minute, we're all alone again, our drinks in front of us.

"You're quite popular," I note, chuckling. "All the ladies here seem quite taken with you."

"I told you I'm hot." He shoves a hand through his hair, smirking at me, before laughing and dropping his hand to pick up his drink to take a sip. "Verna knew me as a little boy. I've always been her fave person, or so she says. Told me I needed to settle down and give her some pseudo-grand-babies. I believe she and my father had a thing going on after mom died, but they said nothing to me, if so."

"Ah." I pick up my drink, and Quinton holds up his glass as if in a toast. "What?"

His eyes grow serious, the next words out of his mouth soft and unexpected. "To our first date. And, a birthday wish to Zander."

My breath catches, my mouth going dry as I stare at him, and his gaze never wavers from mine. I can't believe he remembered. It's only when he speaks that I realize I've said the words out loud.

"Why wouldn't I remember, Evie?" He reaches across the table and covers my free hand with his. "Being interested in you means I should know all the things about you I can."

He's right. I know he's right, but I'm still shocked by it. Dominick was the only person in my life before who noted the small things...

I shake my head out of that train of thought, drumming up a smile for Quinton and his efforts to please me, and clink my glass against his. We both drink after that, and he keeps his hand on mine until our dinner arrives.

And wouldn't you know, I have the best tater tots of my life, just like he promised.

The quality ties right up there with Quinton's company on one of the hardest days of every year for me.

CHAPTER 24

Quinton parks the car, and once we've both gotten out, he walks me to my door.

We stand in front of it facing one another, and I suppose it's like in the movies, where we're both awkward teenagers unsure of what to do next. Not that I would know personally; I've never been with anyone except Dominick, and we certainly never did the whole dating thing like this.

Nervous, I reach into my purse and pull out the keys, turning to the knob to unlock it and let myself in.

"Thanks for tonight," I mumble, sliding the key into the hole before looking back at Quinton, who is staring at me with an amused smile. "Why're you staring at me like that?"

"You seem in a hurry to escape my company."

"Oh." I drop my hands to my side, leaving the keys

dangling in the lock as I turn toward him again, and hold my hands up in a helpless gesture. "I'm not. I just don't know what I'm supposed to do. I've never gone on a date before."

"But you were married..."

"Yeah." I look at my door, back at his face, then place my hand on the knob again before suggesting, "We can talk inside if you want. I don't enjoy standing in front of my place like this."

He slides his hands into his pockets and nods. "Sure. I'd love to hear how you were married yet never dated."

I lead, and he follows, sitting on the couch while I shut the door and put my purse in its place before grabbing two sodas from the fridge. Handing him one, I take a seat beside him, and after taking a sip, laugh.

"This is the first time I've let anyone inside my apartment."

Quinton lifts a brow, taking a sip of the soda in his right hand, and placing his left arm along the back of the couch. His hand rests on the top right behind my neck, and I'm sure he wants to touch me but doesn't as he says, "I suppose I should feel lucky then."

Yes... lucky.

I hate that word most of the time.

"Dominick and I never truly went on a date." I take a sip of my soda, which has me licking my lips and him staring at them in response. I drop my eyes to my lap and roll the can between my hands as I continue. "We went out as friends when we first met, and one year after we met, he proposed. We went from friends to engaged; then we found out I was pregnant, and we got married when I was three months along. And before him... well, he was my first everything."

"Wow. No wonder you seem so innocent. You kind of are."

A snort of laughter escapes me as I lift my eyes to his face. "Please. I'm anything but innocent."

He leans forward, placing his soda on the table, before turning to me and removing mine to do the same. Then, with a gentle smile, he takes my hands in his.

"You've been through a lot, that's true." He looks around my apartment which is, admittedly, rather bare considering I've been here two years. "Is this your first place of your own, ever?"

"Yeah."

"I can tell." He nods at the surrounding room. "You have the essentials and nothing else. You live here, but this isn't your home. It's just where you're existing. Why haven't you made it yours?"

I pull my hands from his and scowl, even though I can't deny what he's saying. The doctor in the psych ward had told me the same thing when I asked why I couldn't stay there, telling me I was existing and not living.

"I don't know."

My answer is honest, and as his eyes bore into mine, I fight the urge to shift under his gaze. It continues for several moments, and I'm not sure what to say. Or if I should say anything at all. And when one of us finally speaks, it's he who does so.

"I'd like to date you, Evie."

His statement doesn't surprise me. We both know that's what he's wanted for a year now. "I know."

He lifts a hand, using it to tuck a few stray strands of hair behind my ear, before sliding his hand down to rest gently on my jaw and neck, his thumb caressing my cheek. "I like you."

"I know." I swallow, unable to ignore the small tingles of pleasure his touch gives me because it's been too long since someone has touched me this way. I'm not sure if I want him to stop, or keep going, and I see his eyes darken at my acknowledgment.

"What are you afraid of, Evie?" His words are a whisper as he keeps our eyes locked. "Or do you not like me as well? I can handle it if that's how you feel. Just tell me."

Shaking my head, I say, "I think you're a great guy..."

"But?"

My smile is self-deprecating as I give him an honest answer. "Well, my marriage crashed and burned. Hard. I don't think I'm good at relationships—"

His thumb moves from stroking my cheek to covering

my lips, cutting off my words as he grins at me. "Evie. You're talking to a man who gave up on dating because it was too difficult for him to understand and navigate. But it won't stop me from taking a chance with you." He leans his face toward mine, getting close enough he can press his mouth against the corner of my lips, sending a shiver of awareness straight through me. "You went through a lot, but so much has changed in the last two years. If you like me, take a gamble on me. I won't let you down."

"It's not you I'm worried about, Quinton."

Moving close until our bodies touch like our lips just had, both of his hands come up to my face, cupping a cheek in each warm hand while chuckling. He locks his gaze on mine as he states, "I'm not worried about you either, Evie. I have a good idea of what I'm getting with you; you should have more faith in yourself." With hooded eyes, his focus drops to my lips. "Tell me you'll date me."

As I stare at him, and he continues to regard my lips with blatant desire, anxiety rises at the decision I have to make right now. I know I can tell him I can't and he will back off, but it's not true. I like him; I can date him. He's smart, educated, funny, a hard worker, and gorgeous. He could have his pick of women, yet he wants me, and why shouldn't I give us a chance?

A small part of me really wants it because I'm lonely. Not a big part, but enough I'm hesitant to give into the desire to be close to anyone. I don't want to fuck up; I don't want to get in over my head and lose it like I did before. And that's what I need him to know, just in case.

"If I say yes, promise me something," I respond on a soft breath, clasping my hands in my lap as his gaze lifts to meet mine once more.

He smiles, eyes filled with a desire he's been trying to hide as much as possible for a while now, and nods. "Anything."

"Promise me you'll back off if I ask you to, and that it won't interfere with our work relationship."

"Absolutely." He doesn't even hesitate in his response before he lowers his voice and asks, "May I kiss you now?"

All I can manage is a small nod, my mouth going dry while my heart beats faster and harder. I lick my lips to wet them and the motion along with my agreement has Quinton covering my mouth with his in one fluid move. One of his hands cups the back of my neck while the other drops and wraps around my waist, his strong hold intent on bringing our bodies flush against each other.

Not wanting my hands trapped between us, I bring them up and around his neck. He groans with pleasure into my mouth, his tongue sweeping in to deepen our kiss as our clothed bodies get as close as they can possibly be.

His hand on my waist instantly drops to the edge of my silk blouse, teasing the skin just underneath with the tips of his fingers before he slides his hand up to the center of my bare back, resting his hot palm there. I can feel it, but I'm mostly focused on the way his kiss makes my body come alive.

It's been a while since I've felt this way. Over two years since I've even kissed anyone, and now, Quinton is the second man to ever have his lips on mine in my life. The compulsion to compare him with Dominick is overwhelming, but I shove it down and aside because there is no point in doing such a thing. In many ways, I'm a much different person now than I was before, more in tune with myself and my feelings, and I've grown a lot from the insecure and lost girl I used to be.

However, it's clear Quinton knows what he's doing as his tongue engages in a soft, sweet battle with mine. The pleasure one stroke sends down my spine has my chest involuntarily pushing against his as my arms tighten around his neck, and in one swift movement, he's got me straddling his lap. His hand left my back to move my body into position, but soon it's returned, yet he doesn't touch me anywhere else.

His hand on my neck spears into my hair as he grabs hold of it, his firm grip tilting my head to intensify the kiss and growls into my mouth, his arousal hard and begging for attention between us as it strains against its barrier. Even though I know it's too soon, and it's not the right time, the feel of him between my legs makes me wish he would just undo his pants, reach underneath my skirt to push my panties aside, and give us both what our bodies are pleading for right this instant.

And for an insane second, as his hand drops to cup my ass, and he grinds our lower bodies together, I think he will do exactly that.

But no.

He drags his mouth away from mine, both of us panting hard while staring at one another for what seems like forever, until finally he grins at me and says, "Yep. I will look forward to doing that a lot."

Not waiting for me to reply, he gives me another soft, sweet kiss on the lips before lifting me off his lap and setting me beside him on the couch. Then, he stands up and with a slight tinge of regret in his voice declares, "It's time for me to leave before those beautiful lips of yours convince me otherwise." He holds out a hand for me, and I stand as I take it, his eyes filling with concern as he stares down at me. "Are you all right?"

He's not asking if I'm okay about the kiss. No, he wants to know if I'll be fine if he leaves me alone now, and I like that he cares enough to ask. A part of me wants to ask him to stay, but know that when he stays in my bed, it shouldn't be because of what day it is or how lonely I am; it should be because I want him there.

"I'm all right," I whisper, giving his hand a squeeze. "Thanks for tonight."

"My pleasure." Leaning in, he kisses the corner of my

mouth, winks at me while releasing my hand, and glances back at me as he opens the door. "See you in the morning."

"Yes, you will."

The moment my front door shuts and I'm all alone, my phone rings. It's Dominick's name on the screen when I finally fish it out from my purse.

And for the first time in two years, I don't answer his call.

Instead, I go to bed with a smile on my face, feeling as if I'm living and not merely existing for the first time in a while.

CHAPTER 25

THE LOUD POUNDING ON THE DOOR JERKS ME OUT OF A dream I'm unable to remember, and it's even more confusing when I roll over to look at the clock only to discover it's three a.m.

Who the hell is here at this time of night?

Rolling out of bed, I slip into my robe and belt it as I walk toward the living room, whoever the hell it is knocking loudly once more.

Looking through the peephole, I'm only able to see the top of someone's bent head, so I call out, "Who is it?"

"Evie," Dominick's voice responds as he looks up at the same time to make sure I know it's him as if I wouldn't recognize his voice anywhere. "Open the door."

The part of me that always went along with him wants to just let him in, but that's one beautiful thing about divorce. Divorce means I don't have to do a damn thing.

"No. It's three in the morning, and I was sleeping. Go home."

"You didn't answer the phone earlier." His voice is accusatory, the scowl on his face clear as he glares at me through the peephole. "Not only do I know you ignored me, but I also had to worry about you on top of everything else."

"Well, don't." I stop looking out and take a step back from the door. "I don't need you to worry about me anymore. I'm fine. We're not together, I'm not your responsibility. Go home, Dominick."

Of course, he ignores me. "Please let me in. We need to talk."

If I didn't know Dominick well, I'd say he's almost begging but he's not. The demand, although framed as a request, tells me he won't go away until I let him in and talk to him as he wishes. With a heavy sigh of resignation, I unlock the deadbolt and open the door, stepping back as he steps inside before shutting it behind him.

This is the first time I've seen him since the day he handed me the completed divorce papers two years ago, and he hasn't changed a bit, while I'm a far cry from the insecure, inexperienced girl he first met.

Everything about him is familiar; his dark hair the same length, his darker eyes with their banked emotions, and his never-wavering confidence. A part of me wants him to open his arms so I can step into the warmth and comfort I know they will give me — an urge I squelch as quickly as it arises.

With a lift of my chin, I inquire, "What was so important you couldn't wait, Dominick?"

"Why did you ignore my call, Evie?" He takes a few steps closer until we're mere inches apart, making my heart race in the way it always has in his presence and crosses his arms as he asks, "Well? First time in two years that you've not answered when I called. And on this day of all others. Why?"

I hate how his eyes bore into mine as I swallow hard, trying to get rid of the lump in my throat at the pain in his eyes, and only answer him when I've torn my gaze away. "I didn't want to talk, and I was busy."

"I see."

That's all he says, the silence swiftly falling between us, long enough I want to scream in frustration because his disappointment in my answer is palpable. I'm not sure what I'm supposed to say, yet when it becomes apparent that he will not speak first, I drag my apologetic gaze back to his.

"I'm sorry, but I've... I'm seeing someone. We went out, I had a good day despite what day it was, and I didn't want to talk."

A myriad of emotions flicker over his face at what I've said. From his initial glower to stunned, before going straight back to disappointment. But it doesn't stay that way for long as his stance relaxes and he slips his hands into his pockets, his expression slipping to neutral as he says, "That's what I've come to speak to you about, actually."

"Oh?"

I can't imagine how he would want to talk to me about my new relationship with Quinton, but his response is something I can honestly say I never expected.

He stares at me, his gaze unwavering as quiet falls between us again, but this time, his eyes give him away. Our years together give me a slight advantage because I see it in his countenance, and whatever he wants to tell me, whatever he's trying to form into words, his fear of my reaction is evident in his eyes.

"I've been dating someone as well—"

Cutting in, and not sure why he had to tell me this in the middle of the night, I say with a tight smile, "Are you? Good for you."

"And," he continues with more force to his voice, glancing away with a swallow before refocusing on my face and softening his tone. "And, we're getting married."

Two years have passed since we split up and both of us moving on was inevitable. Him saying he's getting married shouldn't hurt at all, yet his statement smacks me square in the chest, and my heart twists with a pain I have no right to feel.

I wanted out. I left him. He wanted to make things work between us, and I wouldn't let him.

None of this stuff I remind myself of eases the fact he's moved on in such a small amount of time — and to the point of marriage, no less — causing me to stab a finger at the door, tears filling my eyes as I whisper, "Get out."

"Evie—"

"No." My interruption is a snap as I step toward the door and grab the handle without looking at him. "I don't want to talk to you so please leave."

"You've no right to be angry, Evie," he reminds me even while walking toward the door as I've told him to. "But I thought you had a right to know."

"Just go." Turning the knob, I step back while opening the door and keep my gaze averted, hoping the lack of response will make him leave without saying anything else.

But it doesn't, of course. He moves until I'm surrounded by him — the warmth from his body and his familiar scent invading my senses — and it takes everything I have to stay passive when he places a hand on my shoulder.

A tumult of emotions join in on the assault from his invasion of my personal space, a tear slipping out and down my cheek as his other hand comes down to rest on the opposite shoulder, and he presses a kiss to the top of my head. "I want nothing more than for your happiness, Evie.

And I'm glad you're doing well. Call me if you need anything, or want to talk. Anytime, sweetheart."

He's gone after that, tugging the handle from my grasp as he shuts the door gently behind him, and leaves me standing here trying to catch my breath.

And angry, but not at him. I'm mad at myself for the undesirable way I feel about him building a new life with someone who isn't me. He's right; I have no right to be angry because I asked for a divorce and he gave me one, even though he made it clear how much it would hurt him.

What did I expect? I pushed him out of my life, told myself he deserved to find someone else who would make him happy, and that's exactly what he's done.

I head back to bed, the small amount of happiness Quinton had brought out earlier now squashed by the undesirable pain caused by Dominick's announcement.

CHAPTER 26

Years have passed since I've seen or heard from my mother.

She became angry with me when I left home at eighteen and cut me from her life without so much as a goodbye, so having a man claiming to be her attorney standing on my doorstep early the next morning is strange and random.

Unwanted, too, but when he gives me a sad smile, I understand he's here to tell me she's died.

The fact I feel nothing while recognizing she's gone means nothing; my whole life with her had been miserable, and there was never any love lost between us.

When he takes a seat on my sofa, I sit in the chair off to the side, and the man who introduced himself as Mister Hull speaks first.

"Miss Newman, I'm sorry to inform you that your mother passed away a little shy of six months ago."

Both my brows lift at how much time has passed and wonder why he's here now after all this time. "Uh, thank you, but it's all right. My mother and I weren't close at all."

He nods as if unsurprised, and I suppose he is. I doubt if a parent and child are close that one would miss the funeral or be unaware of the other's death.

Clearing his throat, he says, "Yes, well, although I became your mother's counsel shortly before she died, I wasn't prepared for the number of complications I discovered upon her death. That's why it's taken me so long to contact you."

"What complications?"

"How much do you know about your mother's history, Miss Newman?"

"Not much," I respond with a shrug, wondering why this matters at all, but humoring him. "She never talked about her past, and the one time I dared to ask, she made it clear I was never to ask again."

He stares at me for a moment, swallowing hard as he nods again, and then reaches for his briefcase. Pulling out a small stack of papers, he puts the briefcase down and clutches the papers in his hands while looking at me once more. "The thing is, Miss Newman, is that your mother wasn't who she claimed to be your whole life."

"Uh, I'm sorry. What?"

His eyes fill with sympathy — or is that pity? — at my apparent confusion. "I will explain, but let me finish before you say anything; any question you might have may be answered in the information I'm about to give you."

"All right."

"Your mother listed herself as Terry Newman on your birth certificate, Miss Newman. But that was a false identity. Although we found the forged documents in her things, it remains unclear how she got them."

He frowns when I suck in a breath at this but keeps going after I remain silent as he asked. "The false identity helped her flee from her marital home, where she was married to one Jackson Lockhart, about a month before your birth. Although they searched for your mother, eventually the investigation into her disappearance ended, and ten years after she left, your father had your mother declared dead in absentia as there had been no proof during those intervening years that she remained living or had given birth to the child."

My heart had picked up at the mention of my mother being married and continues to beat hard as I stare at him, my mouth hanging open in both disbelief and pure shock. I'm not even able to process what he's said before he leans forward and holds out the papers to me.

Snapping my mouth shut, I take the stack from his hand, understanding he wants me to go through them one by one. As I stare at the amended birth certificate resting on the top, Mister Hull says in a soft voice, "Your name remains the same, and you are the only person who has the power to change your name if you wish. However, your birth certificate now lists the correct names of both your parents — Jackson Lockhart and Meryl Trenton."

Even though I'm listening to him, all I can do is stare in shock at *my father's name* on this piece of paper which explains everything about my life, such as why my mother thought people were after us.

It also, however, fills me with plenty of unanswered questions; most of which I'll get no answers to because my mother's dead and only she could respond to the fundamental one of why she left him?

Mister Hull clears his throat. "I have informed your father of your existence and he wishes to meet you. That is, only if you want to."

My heart beats faster, thinking of my father spending over twenty-five years believing his wife and unborn child deceased, and me, spending my entire life believing my father abandoned me without a second thought to a crazy mother.

For a moment, I don't answer Mister Hull, going through the stack piece-by-piece — local newspaper clippings about her disappearance and more, along with her final death certificate — until the last one. Catching my breath, I stare down at the photo of my father and mother, standing next to each other and smiling wide in front of a house with a sold sign on it.

My eyes grow wet with unshed tears at seeing my father for the first time. We look alike, down to the red hair atop our heads, and I no longer wonder why it seems like my mother didn't love me — every day my existence probably reminded her of my father, the man she had disappeared on without a trace.

The 'why' question bothers me more with each passing moment. Lifting my gaze to Mister Hull, I stack the papers nice and neat again before grimacing. "There's nothing in her papers saying why she left like she did?"

"No, there wasn't. Mister Lockhart insists he will answer any questions you have, in whatever way you desire to communicate with him. He understands he is a complete stranger to you and doesn't wish to push you into meeting him if you don't want to."

I don't even have to think about what to do next because there's nothing I want more at this moment than to get to know my father.

"Tell him I would love to meet him."

MISTER HULL LEAVES AFTER GIVING ME HIS NUMBER and assuring me he'll call when he has more information from my father about when he would like to meet. This after I told him my work will need advance notice of time off, so at least two weeks before is necessary.

Quinton knocks on my door minutes later, and with my wet hair in my hand, I open the door and let him in.

"Give me a few more minutes, I'm running behind." I head toward the bathroom without waiting for his response.

I don't know what to say to him or how to explain what's going on. He doesn't know much about my childhood or what my mother was like; we've never discussed it.

No, the only person who knows everything is Dominick, and now I have to decide whether to tell him what's going on or not. After last night, the last thing I want to do is talk to him, because the fact he's getting married bothers me the same this morning as it had last night.

And so I'm bad at relationships. I've agreed to date Quinton, that means I need to tell him, right?

Ugh. Of course, I do. I try not to think about my past because it's irrelevant now, but he will need to know — especially since I will be taking time off work to go meet my father who lives thousands of miles away.

Quinton appears in the doorway as I finish blow drying my hair, and leans against the door frame, watching me put on my mascara. He crosses his arms over his chest with a laugh and says, "There hasn't been a day since you started working with me where you've been late. Everything all right?"

"My mother's attorney arrived earlier to inform me she died six months ago."

I cap the mascara and grab my eyeliner, trying not to laugh when his face goes from amused to incredulous as he takes a step closer to me, putting his hands on my shoulders. "Six months ago and you're just now finding out? Holy shit. Do you need to take the day off?"

Shaking my head, I laugh and shrug off his hands, leaning forward to put on the eyeliner while he stands scowling behind me. "Your concern is sweet, but there's a reason I didn't know she was dead. We weren't that close and after what the attorney told me, I'm glad she's gone."

His eyebrows shoot up as he takes a step back. "Evie—"

I wave my hand in a dismissive gesture as I put the makeup away and turn to him. "I'll explain in the car. Just let me get my purse and we can go."

He doesn't say anything, but by the time we pull into the parking lot at work, he stops the car and turns it off before blowing out a harsh breath. "Wow. That's a huge secret for her to keep her whole life, from everyone."

"Yep. She was a horrible woman through and through."

He reaches across the center console and grabs my head, bringing it up to his mouth to kiss the back, his expression sad. "Evie, I had no idea your childhood was that awful. I'm sorry."

"Don't be. I rarely speak of it, and I'm not angry at her for that anymore. Now I've got something brand new to be pissed about — her deliberately keeping me from knowing my father or the rest of my family."

"You have every right to be angry. It's clear your mother wasn't mentally stable in the slightest." He releases my hand and pulls the keys from the ignition. "Let me know when you need to leave and, please, take as much time as you need. Your job will wait for you."

"I know. And thanks."

"You're welcome." He leans over, his face and mouth inches from mine as he murmurs, "Now, how about a kiss before we go in and I have to keep my hands to myself?"

At my nod, he presses a soft, sweet peck to my mouth, so different from the hungry lip lock last night that when he draws away, I sigh a little in disappointment.

"I know," he says with a chuckle, lifting a hand to caress my cheek with the pad of his thumb before pulling away and running that same hand through his hair. "I haven't played hooky in a long time, but I'm tempted to with you today."

The fact he would skip work for me is amusing enough I ask, "Oh? What would we do?"

"I can't say," he responds while opening the door, tossing me a wink over his shoulder as he turns to exit. "It's not appropriate for the workplace."

My face flushes at that and remains that way while we

walk inside, where we work as if there's nothing between us, but the occasional glances from co-workers tells me we aren't fooling anyone.

And by the end of the day, it's confirmed when Jessica knocks on Quinton's door, grinning when we both look up from the papers we're going through before saying, "It's late, you two. Head home and canoodle or something; there's always tomorrow."

Quinton is the first to speak because except for the kiss outside, we've always behaved professionally at work, even if he has joked about dating me before in front of them. "How—?"

"Please." Jessica rolls her eyes and shoves her hands into her pockets with a burst of laughter. "We've been taking bets and y'all just won me a hundred dollars. Not fooling anyone. Night!"

She whirls around and walks away before either of us can reply, both staring at each other dumbfounded for a second before Quinton grin and sets his papers aside.

Then, without a word, he plucks me from my seat and places me in his lap, his hand sliding around to cup the back of my neck while his lips cover mine with a delicious kiss that makes my toes curl.

It's the perfect ending to the work day.

FOLLOWING THAT EVENING, QUINTON AND I continue to keep things professional at work. In truth, I do a better job of it than he does, often because he will put his hand around my waist without thinking about it, or lean in to kiss my cheek when I've brought something into his office to discuss with him.

It's sweet.

Well, he's nice and so easy to get along with, which unfortunately leads me to think about how my relationship with Dominick had been similar at first, although Quinton is less dominant and more soft at heart.

And speaking of Dominick...

Nearly three weeks have passed since the night he showed up on my doorstep, and I haven't heard from him. He has called regularly since our divorce, but perhaps now that he's informed me of his upcoming wedding and knows I'm dating someone, he no longer finds it necessary.

But tomorrow, I'm heading to meet my father, and because Dominick was my rock for so long, I've decided he needs to know what's going on.

So, picking up the phone, I dial his number and wait with my heart in my throat as it rings.

He answers on the third one with more than a little surprise in his voice. "Evie. Is everything all right?"

"Hi, Dominick. Yes, everything is fine."

Now that he's on the phone, and I hear his voice, I have the incredible urge to tell him I dialed the wrong number and hang up. Even after two years, everything about him reminds me of Zander, and although it's only an ache now instead of a gaping wound, I want to burst into tears and have him wrap his arms around me like always.

Because that's what Dom is to me — comfort and familiarity. Security. But no longer, especially since he's getting married to someone else.

The reminder of that fact has me squaring my shoulders as he chuckles softly and speaks into the long silence.

"Did you need something, sweetheart?"

"You probably shouldn't call me that," I bite back without thinking, only to bite my lip and slam my eyes shut in embarrassment. "I mean, I'm sure your fiancée doesn't want you calling other women pet names."

"Habit." His response is short and filled with more irritation than affection now. "Did you call for a reason, Evie, or should I prepare for a continuation of our previous discussion?"

Ignoring his comment, I take a deep breath and say, "Yes, I did. I... I'm leaving tomorrow morning, going out of town to meet... well, to meet my father."

A brief pause, then a mildly confused, "I'm sorry, what?"

Filling him in on the details doesn't take too long and at the end, he says the last thing I would ever expect him to say.

"You shouldn't go by yourself, Evie. I will join you."

"What? No."

"Evie, sweet—" He releases a sigh of frustration I can practically feel through the phone as he cuts off. At the sound of his hand covering the phone while his voice becomes muffled almost has me hanging up because I bet his fiancée is there, but I don't since he comes back on the line quickly. "Like I said, I'll go with you. This isn't something you should do without some support, not with everything that's happened."

"I've been fine for a while now, Dominick. What makes you think I won't be okay with this? I'm choosing this, it doesn't even compare to..." My throat clogs up because I can't even say the words out loud. "Thanks for the offer, but I can do this on my own. I just thought you should know."

"Evie—"

I interrupt him with a forceful, "Goodnight, Dominick," and hang up the phone before he can say anything else.

Then, I shut it off, put it on the table by the door, and grab my keys before heading up to Quinton's apartment.

"Just in time for dinner," Quinton says as he opens his door, letting me walk through before shutting it, and pulling me into his arms for a brief kiss. "Good timing."

"I aim to please."

He laughs and releases me from his hold with a nod toward the table. "Take a seat while I get everything from the kitchen."

"I can help."

"Nope. It'll only take a minute, promise."

Sitting down at the table, it isn't long before he's seated across from me, and he's smiling while telling me stories about his days in college as we're eating.

Then, once we're finished, he removes everything from the table and takes it back to the kitchen, shaking his head when I offer to help him wash them. He comes back a moment later, grabs my hand, and leads me over to the couch, where we both sit down in our usual positions — him with his arm around my shoulders and me cuddled into his side.

"So," he says with a deep breath in and a rough one out. "Did you tell him?"

"Yep. I figured he would only wish me luck, but he offered to go with me."

"Really? How nice of him."

That's the one thing I like about Quinton. He says that, and he means it; there isn't a stiffening of his body, nor do I get the impression he's threatened by Dominick at all. No, he genuinely believes Dominick's offer was a nice one to make, and it makes me like him even more.

"I told him no, even though he insisted I should have some support there with me."

Quinton doesn't respond, and he doesn't have to because he said the same thing to me a few days ago after I told him all about my breakdown following Zander's death. Yet once I assured him I would be fine, he took me at my word, unlike Dominick, who apparently believes I will lose it again at any second.

"Something tells me I will find him on my doorstep in the morning."

At that, he gazes down at me with amusement in his eyes and lifts a hand to cup my cheek. "Well, you can stay the night with me and leave him to cool his heels come morning."

"Have you decided this is the best way to get me in your bed?" We've not done more than kiss and cuddle since we began dating, leaving part of me to wonder why he hasn't tried to sleep with me since I believe he wants to as much as I do. But then I don't know what to do except laugh softly when he frowns and drops his hand. "I'm just teasing, Quinton."

"I know. And I would love nothing more than to sleep with you, Evie."

Uh oh. "But?"

"Not a but. More like, it might be best we wait until after you return from meeting your father."

"Why?"

"Because that's what you should focus on. Your father not being in your life — whether you thought him an entirely different sort of person your whole life — is a big deal, and may have affected you in ways not discovered yet. Doing this will bring all those things to the surface, and we should take the next step after you've dealt with this."

Even though I understand where he's coming from, my eyes fill with tears anyway as I wrap my arms around his neck and kiss his cheek. "Don't I get a say in this?"

"You've had a say since we met." He clears his throat and lowers his gaze to my mouth for a brief moment before focusing on my eyes again. "I'm not going anywhere, Evie, and I think you're an amazing woman. However, you're not ready for serious, not yet, and sex with you would be significant for both of us."

He's right, it would, yet I'm more than a little disappointed because I don't see this the same way he does. I feel ready; otherwise, I would've stopped this after our first date.

His words are something I question the rest of the evening while we watch a movie and eat popcorn, and then later, as we curl up next to each other in his bed to spend our first night together.

But no answers are forthcoming as I lie there with just the sweet warmth of Quinton's arm around me as we both drift off to sleep.

"Your leg is touching mine."

One hour into the flight and I want to strangle Dominick, who, just as I told Quinton he would, sat outside my apartment waiting for me to head to the airport this morning.

Insisting he was going on my trip with me, he somehow managed to secure a seat on my flight, too. Then, once on it, he convinced the person who originally had the seat next to me to switch with him, and now I'm stuck with his big body invading my space in these tiny seats.

"Quit whining, Evie," he says with a glare in my direction. "You're the one who chose economy seats with no space when you can more than afford better ones."

"Wrong. These are what I can afford on my salary."

"You know I'm not talking about the money from your job."

"Stop talking to me." Pulling my headphones from my bag, I put one bud in my ear and hold the second near the other as I ignore his reference to the money from our divorce. "I told you I didn't want you here, and you didn't listen."

"And you acting like a child is exactly why I didn't."

"You thinking you always know what's best for me and ignoring my wishes is why we're divorced."

"No, sweetheart, giving into your desires is exactly the reason we're divorced. Perhaps I should've put you over my knee instead."

My turn to glower at him, the idea of him putting me over his knee and spanking me like a child heating up my face because I'm strangely turned on by the image. Shoving the other bud into my ear without responding, I turn my face to the window while switching on my music player to drown out any noise except that of the musical kind, and try not to let him see how much he affects me.

He looks good. Hell, he smells amazing as always, and

I lean my body toward the window to keep from touching him, including angling both my legs.

We don't speak again for the rest of the flight, but I've never been more aware of his presence than I am right now and do not know how I will deal with him being by my side during this whole trip.

❧

DOMINICK RENTS A CAR WHEN WE ARRIVE AT THE airport and inserts my father's address into the GPS before exiting the carpark.

My father lives an hour's drive away, and nothing makes me happier than when Dominick turns on the radio, essentially leaving me to my own thoughts without me even asking him.

Gazing out the window, there's nothing more than miles and miles of brilliant green trees lining the highway, and not for the first time, I let my mind wander, thinking about what my father will be like.

I could've spoken to him on the phone before coming here, yet I chose not to. Something bothered me about getting to know him that way, wanting to talk to my father for the first time while looking into his face, and felt relieved after the attorney told me my father understood perfectly.

From everything I've learned, he's in his late fifties, and

five years after my mother disappeared, he began a new relationship with a woman named Colleen. He and Colleen had a son they named William — making him my half-brother — and he turned eighteen years old earlier this year. They later married after my mother was declared dead and have remained together since.

Honestly, I'm glad he hadn't ended up alone after my mother just up and disappeared on him. He spent years looking for her, and I don't believe him giving up meant he loved her any less; just that zero signs of her for five years meant he probably would find none.

He found happiness where he could, considering the circumstances and now, he would have his first child in his life, too.

Smiling at the thought, I relax for the first time today and close my eyes to rest them until we get there.

CHAPTER 28

"Evie," Dominick whispers in my ear to wake me, pressing a kiss to my cheek before pulling away as he taps me softly on the shoulder. "We're here, sweetheart."

Sitting up from where the side of my head presses against the window, I rub at my eyes before opening them and gasp at the beautiful house in front of me.

It's the same one my mother and father stood in front of in that picture Mister Hull showed me. A little older, but no worse for wear; in fact, it appears to have had work done on it recently.

"Thanks," I say to Dominick while unbuckling my seat belt, opening my door and getting out before he can say anything else.

Shutting the door, I stare at the house, the sound of Dominick getting out of the car barely noticeable, and my breath catches as the front door opens.

Three people exit the house, but I've got eyes for one person only, and as my father walks down the steps, the urge to run toward him is powerful.

Intense enough that when he stops at the bottom and merely stares at me with a tentative smile, I give in to the compulsion, taking off full speed in his direction.

He opens his arms, only to wrap me in his warm embrace when my body practically collides with his, both of us shaking as the magnitude of our emotions takes over.

I don't know how long we stand there, sobbing in each other's arm while the people who love us most stand by witnessing it, but eventually my father draws back with a smile exactly like the one that reflects back at me in the mirror and says, "Welcome home."

This moment is more than I imagined it would be, and for the first time in my life, his words make me feel as if some place is truly my home.

"Thank you." Wiping at my eyes, I return his smile and clasp my hands in front of me as he turns toward the other two coming down the steps.

"This is my wife, Colleen," he says with a loving glance at his wife, "and our son, William."

Colleen steps forward with what sounds like a small held-back sigh, pulling me into a tight hug before stepping back and laughing. "Nice to meet you, honey. You're a spitting image of your father, as we knew you would be."

"You did?"

"Yes. Look at William, you two could be twins! Strong genes."

"Mom," William objects with a roll of his eyes before stepping forward and holding out his hand for me to take. "I would hug you, but I don't enjoy hugging people, and only let my mom get away with it because otherwise, she'll cry."

Taking his hand, I shake it and smile at his candor. "No problem. I think that's why I let her hug me, too."

William and my father laugh, while Colleen winks at me before gazing over my shoulder and asks, "Who is this with you?"

My face grows heated at realizing I totally forgot about Dominick, only to jump when I turn to look at him and discover him standing less than half a foot behind me. He steps forward to introduce himself before I can do it.

"I'm Dominick, her ex-husband."

I hadn't had time to tell Mister Hull that Dominick was coming, so they wouldn't have had any idea.

But although Colleen's mouth forms an 'o' of surprise, my father merely gives a simple nod and takes Dominick's hand to shake it briefly before saying, "Come on inside. I hope you two are hungry. Colleen's outdone herself for lunch."

My stomach takes that perfect moment to growl, everyone laughing as I put my hands on my belly in embarrassment, and then we head inside to eat.

* * *

After we're done eating, Colleen shows Dominick to his room, my father and I head into his study to talk, with William sticking his head in to say, "See ya around."

He's gone before I can say anything, and my father chuckles while sitting behind his desk as I take a seat in the opposite chair. "He's off to work and then back to his dorm. He could have lived at home for his first year of college, but insisted he wanted the whole experience."

"So he came here just to meet me?"

"Yes." His face flushes as he gazes out the window for a second before looking at me once again. "It was an awkward conversation to have with him because he never knew about my previous marriage, let alone everything that happened. But he's had about six months to adjust to the news, which is more than you've had, and I apologize for that."

"Why?"

He tilts his head a little to the side and studies me, reminding me so much of myself that I want to squirm in my chair but resist the impulse. "Mister Hull contacted me the moment he discovered your mother's real identity. He wished to communicate with you immediately, but until we had all the facts, I thought it best not to interrupt your life."

"Well," I reassure him with a smile, "there's no need to apologize. My mother told me my father abandoned us from the time I was little, so that is what I believed until Mister Hull's arrival. Trust me, this isn't something I considered bad news, except for the whole deception on my mother's part."

"I understand you two weren't close."

"Nope. She... she wasn't well my entire childhood. Paranoid really, which is something I understand now. She was afraid you would find us, but the question is, why didn't she want that?"

He leans forward, clasping his hands on his desk and shaking his head. "Truthfully, I wish I understood her actions, but that information died with your mother. Throughout her whole pregnancy, everything seemed perfect. Then one day I returned home from work, and she left me without so much as a note."

"Bizarre, but nothing she did made sense to me as a kid, or even later as an adult."

"Worse than bizarre. For a while, they suspected me of murdering her." At my gasp, he laughs and holds up a hand. "Oh, not openly. They had no proof or anything substantial to back up such a claim. They did their jobs and looked for her, but in reality, many believed her long dead, and no protests of my innocence would convince them otherwise."

I had suffered from my mother's actions, but my father had experienced worse at the hands of a woman he loved. None of this is my fault, yet I want to say sorry, anyway.

Instead, I say, "Well, you're innocent, and now everyone knows it. Plus, she may have robbed us all these years, but not any longer. She can't hurt either of us anymore."

"True." He pauses, studying me again for a moment, and then asks with a sad smile, "So tell me why your ex-husband watches you as if you've hung the moon and you act as if he isn't even here right by your side."

Rubbing my hands together over and over in my lap, I drop my gaze from his with a frown. "I don't think he looks at me that way."

"He does. But you're divorced. Why? Because of your son?"

My eyes fly to his, wide with surprise until... "Oh. Mister Hull told you about Zander."

"Yes, he did. And I'm sorry you went through such a heartbreaking experience. Losing a child never gets easier, not even with time. The ache is always there."

Sniffling, I wipe at my eyes and nod, acknowledging that if anyone knows how I feel, it's him. But unlike our case, my son will never return to me. "Yes. It's been two years, and I miss him as much as ever. And Dominick... well, I don't know. If you know about Zander, then you know what happened after he died."

"I don't. Mister Hull wasn't privy to that information. You may tell me if you like, but don't feel as if you have to."

"Oh no, it's okay. I had postpartum depression after

Zander's birth, yet I ignored it, not realizing wasn't normal to feel so disconnected from my child. It wasn't diagnosed until after he died, which it was too late by then. And after... well, I lost it after Zander died. I blamed Dominick, and it wasn't his fault, but that didn't matter.

I pulled away no matter how hard he tried to connect with me and eventually it got to the point I resented him, along with hating how it appeared like our son's death hadn't affected him."

I reach out and take the tissue my father offers me, his eyes filled with understanding and warmth as I continue. "One year after he died, I thought he didn't even remember what day it was, and I drove him up to the place where we discovered I was pregnant, and asked him for a divorce. I was hysterical and ended up stabbing him before fleeing, only to crash the car and lose my memory for a few months after."

He nods while I dab at my eyes as if this doesn't shock him at all. "And the divorce?"

"After I regained my memory, he said he didn't care. That he knew I was unwell and shouldn't have approached me while I held the knife. He asked me to try until what would've been our son's second birthday, but we went to counseling, and I was finally honest about everything. I just couldn't do it anymore. His death affected me — and therefore my relationship with Dominick — in ways I can't even explain now."

"Grief isn't rational," my father murmurs. "When your mother disappeared while pregnant with you, nothing could comfort me. And I didn't have anyone to share with except for my family, who all loved me but couldn't honestly understand what I was going through. The longer we went without finding her, the deeper my grief went, until I was inconsolable, and had to tell myself you two were dead just to make it through the day. I couldn't bear the thought of life without you two if you were alive and out of my reach."

"I felt that way when I picked up Zander's lifeless body in my arms and knew I couldn't save him."

"Of course, you did. And because you blamed your husband, you couldn't turn to him for comfort, even though he undoubtedly hurt as much as you did. Then he let you go because he didn't want you to hurt anymore, even if he loved you. Am I correct?"

Renewed tears flow down my cheeks. "Yes. He didn't want a divorce, but he didn't fight me."

"Nobody wants to be the source of pain for the person they love. You said it's what you wanted, and because he loved you, and the son you shared, he gave it to you."

Although what he's saying isn't anything new, it prompts a question from me. "Would you have let my mother go if she had told you she wanted out instead of running?"

He unclasps his hands and covers his mouth for a

brief moment, his fingers running over his lips before he nods decisively. "I would've tried my hardest to keep our relationship together, but in the end, if that's what she thought was best, I would've given her whatever she wanted, even if it killed me to do so."

That's exactly what I guessed he would say, and it shines a whole new light on the last two years of my life. No, in my entire relationship with Dominick, because he was right on the plane — he always gave me whatever I wanted, even if it led straight to our destruction, to our end.

I never allowed anything else to happen, never truly gave him a choice.

After a brief silence where my mind absorbs his words and that little revelation, I tell him quietly, "It doesn't matter anymore if he loves me."

"Why not?"

"Because he's going to marry someone else."

His gaze is knowing as he smirks like we hadn't just met for the first time mere hours ago. "Do you love him, Evie?"

I blink once, then again, before saying in a whisper, "You're the first person to ever ask me that."

"Well, do you?"

"Honestly, I don't know. I thought I did." I bite my lip, looking down and away in thought before lifting my eyes back to his again as they fill with fresh tears. "When I married him, I thought I loved him, but it wasn't enough to get us through everything. Isn't that what love should be?"

He shakes his head with a light abrupt laugh and rises from his chair, coming around to stand in front of the desk, leaning against it as he speaks. "Love isn't a cure-all, Evie. The passionate beginning is always fantastic, but once it ends, so many confuse it with the love going away. But if it works out, you end up with a deep attachment to the person, the kind where even though you're so angry at your partner for something, the desire for them to pull you into their arms and hold you tight is almost tangible."

My chest tightens with an all too familiar ache at his words, because that is exactly how Dominick makes me feel. The one I experienced the night he came over, wanting him to embrace me moments before he told me he was moving on, and wanting to touch him on the plane even though I was so fucking angry at him pushing his way onto this trip.

He cares, he's always cared, and he knew I would need support here even if I didn't think so. And all I've done since Zander died is punish him for loving me despite every reason I believe he shouldn't.

"Everything you say makes sense," I say to my father while wiping at my cheeks, then stand up and shake my head. "But the issue is with me and always has been. There's something wrong with me because I don't know how to accept his love after everything that's happened. He deserves better than that."

He steps forward and puts a comforting hand on my shoulder. "You're wrong, Evie. There's nothing wrong with you. You're a woman who never felt loved by her mother and thought her father abandoned her. But that's not true. I loved you before you were even born and never stopped, even when I believed the worst, and there's nothing more I want than your happiness."

When I nod, we hug each other again, and then I say, "I think I need to rest for a while."

He lets me go.

And on the way back to my room, I wonder why I believe him when he says he loves me before realizing there's one thing between Dominick and me that isn't between my father and me — history.

CHAPTER 29

After the conversation with my father, it's difficult to avoid acknowledging the truth to his words about Dominick's feelings for me.

Except for the night he came over, we haven't spent any time together in two years, and suddenly we're in the same location with nothing but time.

He sits next to me at dinner, engaging in conversation with not only me but my father and Colleen, too. Like he's been doing it forever while reminding me of how terrific he is at socializing with anyone he comes into contact with — something he's always been great at compared to me.

Half an hour after dinner ends, Colleen and I finish washing the dishes, and my father comes into the kitchen to get her.

"We're old," he jokes, winking at me as he puts his arm around her waist. "Time for bed."

"Goodnight, Evie," Colleen adds as my father leads her out of the room.

"Night."

When they're gone, I finish wiping off the counters and grab a bottle of water out of the fridge, shutting off the light as I walk out of the kitchen toward the room given to me during my stay.

And on the way, I pass the room Dominick's staying in, the closed door surprising me. Figuring he's either not in there, or he doesn't want to talk, I enter my room and climb into bed.

That's when my phone rings, Quinton's name popping up on the screen, and I answer it with a smile in my voice. "Hello."

"Hey, there. How are you doing?"

"I'm great, actually."

"And your father?"

"He's a nice man. We talked for a good bit earlier. It was... amazing and strange simultaneously."

"I can only imagine, and I'm happy it went well." He clears his throat and releases a rough sigh. "It's been a long day, and I'm going to retire early. Turns out there's a lot of work when you're not there."

Through my laughter, I say, "You poor thing. How did you survive before I came on the scene?"

"You know, I don't recall." He joins in my amusement with a chuckle of his own before yawning. "Okay, I just wanted to check in and see how you were. I'm off to shower and then go to bed. Talk tomorrow?"

"Yeah, definitely. I napped a little earlier so I will read for a bit, maybe watch some TV if I can find something interesting."

"Sounds good. Night, Evie."

"Night."

I pull the phone away from my ear, staring at the screen as he disconnects the call, and feel... nothing.

What the hell is wrong with me?

I've been dating him for nearly a month now, and we haven't done more than kiss, but shouldn't I have thought of him during the day? Or missed him?

Yet, I haven't thought about him today more than briefly, and I certainly haven't missed him. And if he hadn't called me, I wouldn't have called him, or even thought it something I should do.

My phone dings in my hand, jerking me out of my thoughts, and I frown at seeing a message from Dominick. He's in the same house, and he's texting me?

I slide the screen to unlock it and tap on the message only to see he's asked me, "Are you awake?"

"Yes." Nearly hitting send, I decide to have a little fun and add, "I mean, I'm pretty sure I am unless I'm sleep-texting. How about you?"

He answers me with his usual lack of humor. "I thought I heard you talking."

"I was. I'm done now. Sorry, did I wake you up?"

"No, I've been up, dealing with work issues. Done now. Want to watch a movie?"

My crazy and unreliable heart — thanks to my discussion with my father earlier — picks up in speed at his invitation. "Depends. Are you going to pick something that will bore me to sleep?"

Instead of answering, he appears in my doorway within a minute and walks into the room wearing nothing more than his usual black silk pajama pants, shutting the door behind him.

"Don't want to wake anyone up," he declares with a wink before going to the other side of the bed and taking a seat beside me, nodding at the remote on the nightstand as I try not to stare at his bare chest like I've never seen it before. "You pick; that way you can't blame me if the movie sucks."

"Sure I can since you're the one who issued the invitation."

Picking up the remote at that, I turn on the TV and press the guide button, slowly scrolling through, trying to find something we can watch.

He isn't checking out the listings with me, though. No, he's staring at me, his eyes practically burning me with their intensity as usual, and it goes on long enough I face him with a lifted brow. "What?"

He mirrors my facial expression for a moment before grinning. "You're different."

Dammit. "No, I'm not."

"I know you, Evie, and when you came out of that room after speaking with your father, I noticed it."

"Like what?" My question — and my tone — is defensive, making me want to wince, but I refrain while glaring at him because he's always like this.

He's correct, though. He knows me, his expression softening as he lifts a hand up to my face and caresses my cheek with the pad of his thumb for an instant before dropping his hand away. "Peace. As if meeting your father soothed a part of your soul that nobody ever would've touched otherwise."

"Of course. He's my father. He's somebody I spent my whole life thinking didn't love me, and in one conversation, I learned it wasn't anything close to the truth. I always knew there was something wrong with my mother and now... now I think I know why my feelings have always been screwed

"I never thought there was anything wrong with you or your emotions, sweetheart. Confused and perhaps a little lost, yes, but not messed up. They're just all locked up inside you and never dealt with in a healthy way."

How quickly the topic turned to me, as always, and with this I frown at him while focusing on the TV again.

"Did you come in here to talk about my father and me or to watch a movie?"

"I will always be more interested in you than a movie, Evie, especially with your emotions written all over your face." He snickers and lifts his hand back to my face, stroking my cheek again before exerting the tiniest bit to pressure to make me look at him once more as he whispers, "Such as right now. You're upset because we're talking about you, and in all the time we've spent together, that wasn't something you enjoyed doing much at all."

I wish he would take his hand away. It's warm and lovely, further proving he remains desirous to me; nothing like the lack of passion from when he kissed me goodbye the day he handed me the divorce papers. That had been all me denying the truth in my mind because I had been so desperate to escape any further pain.

I close my eyes and swallow hard before opening them again to give him a self-deprecating grimace. "There wasn't a lot to say, Dominick. I've always considered myself to be a rather boring person."

"And here I've found you nothing short of fascinating."

"Perhaps you're delusional and should see a doctor about that." When he scowls at that, I copy his expression and lift my hand to his, tugging it away from my face with a sigh. "Look, actually, I have something to say to you."

He tugs his hand free from mine and drops it on the bed between us. "Hm?"

"I realized after speaking to my father earlier that I never apologized to you." At his confused look, I worry my lip for a moment before letting it go and clarifying. "About Zander. I... I blamed you, and I'm sorry. Because blaming you left both of us with nobody to turn to, and even though you tried to stay connected with me, it wasn't going to happen with me holding you responsible for his death. You were fighting a losing battle."

I expect him to say a lot of things when I finish, especially as he sits there watching me with his steady, emotional gaze, but what I don't expect is him saying, "I know."

"You know what?"

"That I fought a losing battle with you from the moment he died. You weren't ready to accept the truth, and the instant you walked out of that counselor's office, I knew our relationship as it was had ended." He scoots closer and cups my cheek in his hand, his mouth curving up in a ghost of a smile. "I wanted to keep fighting, and I would've, yet your pain tore me apart. Losing our son had been bad enough; letting you go was like a second death for me. But I did, all the while hoping your mind would change before long."

Although I want to move into his touch, I don't because of all the conflicting emotions swirling around inside me right now — not to mention how both of us are with other people. Instead I ask the question that's hanging around on my tongue because that might help me decide where to go from here.

It comes out in a quivering whisper, my eyes closing as if doing so will guard against whatever his answer is. "Do you still love me, Dom?"

His response is confident, instant. "Never stopped." My heart pounds as he moves closer, his next words whispered dangerously near to my mouth. "Say the words written all over your face, sweetheart."

"I can't." I open my eyes, gazing straight into his, where all my emotions are reflected back at me. "I know what will happen if I do, and we're both with other people. It wouldn't be right."

Then, for the first time ever, Dominick's face flushes and he draws away, dropping his touch from me as he says, "Ah, it's my turn to apologize now."

"Why? We're not doing anything wrong."

"No." He pinches the bridge of his nose and closes his eyes for a brief second, his mouth turned down into a frown when he meets my gaze again. "I meant, I need to apologize for lying to you."

"Lying? About what?"

"I'm not engaged, sweetheart. Or dating anyone, for that matter."

Both my eyebrows fly up at that, and I cross my arms over my chest, of which the insides tighten with confusion. "What do you mean? You broke up?"

"No. As in, I've been single since the divorce." When my scowl deepens, he sighs and gives a little shrug. "I came over that night because not only had you not answered my call, but I wanted to tell you how I felt, see if you would give our relationship another chance."

My mouth drops open. "You never said any of that."

His jaw tightens, his teeth clenched as he says through them, "I know. You told me you were seeing someone new."

If I weren't shocked as hell, I would laugh at this lack of confidence from him. "Holy shit, Dom. You lied to me because you were jealous?"

Lifting his hands in a helpless gesture, he levels me with heat-filled eyes. "You sounded happier that night, more than all the times we spoke on the phone, and I thought admitting my feelings would confuse things for you."

"So, you decide pissing me off is better, instead?"

At that, he's the one to laugh. "No, actually, your reaction said it all. You wouldn't have reacted that way if you felt nothing for me. But if you hadn't acknowledged those feelings after two years, I didn't believe you would even if I told you, especially since you decided to date someone else."

"So, then what was your plan? To ignore me, since you stopped calling me every day?"

"I would never ignore you, sweetheart. I love you,

which is exactly why I stopped calling you like I used to because I respected your new relationship."

I may not be good at relationships, but I appreciate his thoughtfulness. Something like that never would've occurred to me, and hadn't in fact, because I've never had to deal with it, I suppose.

And now, what do I do with it?

I don't miss Quinton. I like him. We get along well, and maybe it will just take time for things to develop. Yet what if they don't?

What if I tell Dominick it's too late and then my relationship with Quinton doesn't go anywhere?

Not to mention, with loving Dominick, does any of that even matter? Of course, I care about Quinton, and I don't want to hurt him, but otherwise, do I really want to give up on life with Dominick for good when he's the best man I've ever met?

When he loves me despite everything and the same goes for me, even with how anxiety-inducing my feelings are because I fear messing everything up for good?

Dom's watching with such hope as I try to sort through these questions and emotions in my head that I just want him to reach out and decide for me. But he won't because I think we both know I have to decide what to do on my own.

So, I pick up the remote, turn off the TV, and tell him,

"I think it's best if I take some time to think about everything. It's been a long day."

He nods, leaning in to press a kiss to my forehead before pulling away and leaving the bed to walk over to the door. "See you in the morning."

"Yep. Night."

Then, he's gone, and for the first time in two long years, I ache for his arms around me while I sleep.

CHAPTER 30

"Are you ready?" Dominick asks from the doorway, smiling when I drag my gaze away from the book I'm reading to his face, and then he taps his watch when I shake my head. "You forgot about dinner, didn't you?"

"Oh, sorry, I did." Making my page, I put the book on the table beside the bed and run a hand through my hair while standing up. "Give me about five minutes."

"All right. I'll be waiting in the living room."

The moment he walks away, I rush over to my luggage, searching for the one lovely sundress I brought with me. Grabbing it and the white sandals to match, I get dressed, but not in a hurry since we both know it will take me longer than five minutes to get ready.

Dominick asked me to go out to dinner with him at breakfast, my father and Colleen sitting right there beaming at the both of us, and making it clear he had won them over.

He's good at that and always has been. His clients love him. Hell, I've never met a person who doesn't, and turns out I'm no different even though I've told myself otherwise for too long.

So I said yes to dinner because it will help me decide what to do.

I keep thinking it will be an easy decision, but it isn't. I want to believe things will work out this time if given a chance, yet I'm also realistic enough to understand they might not.

How much control do I have? That's the question. Did I have some before, or had all the shit hit the fan at the perfect time when I wouldn't be able to handle it all, or fight back as I needed to?

And how much of that inability came from who I am, or had more of it been because of the depression I suffered from after Zander's birth and compounded by his death?

Worse, what if something like it happens again?

I believe that's what I'm most terrified of — having another child and losing them again in any capacity; does Dominick fear the same thing?

How could he not?

Slipping on the sandals, I smooth down the sundress and walk over to the mirror, running a brush through my hair. Leaving it to hang straight, I put on my usual eyeliner and mascara before grabbing my purse and walking out to the living room.

"There you are," he says, rising from the chair as I enter with a smile. "I've always loved that dress."

"I know. You bought it for me, remember?"

"Of course." He motions toward the door with a sweep of his arm. "Shall we?"

"Yep," I say, smiling at him as I walk past and out the door.

Two minutes later, we're on our way.

* * *

Dominick ends up taking us to this little restaurant by the coast.

"At your father's recommendation," he admitted as we sat down.

Dinner passes in a blur with nothing important being discussed, and after paying, he takes my hand in his as we step back outside.

"Walk with me."

"Okay."

For the first bit, we walk in silence near the water, although not close enough to get wet, and when I notice him mostly staring at me, I lift a brow and smile up at him. "What?"

"I want to show you something."

The old me might've joked that he should be careful

about showing me something in a public place, but not now. I only nod and say, "Okay, what is it?"

He pulls his phone out of his pocket, swiping at it for a few moments before wrapping his arm around my shoulder and tugging me into a side hug before holding his phone in front of us.

On the screen is a pic of Zander, looking up at the camera as he lies in his crib, his fingers in his mouth as usual.

Dom's finger swipes the screen as tears fill my eyes, and a video plays.

"Say Dada," his voice commands to our son, his hand entering view as he reaches down to stroke Zander's cheek, and laughs as our son kicks his feet. "Come on, say dada. Just once before I go to work."

Our son kicks his feet harder, his hands popping out of his mouth as he stares up at his father, and giggles.

"No? You aren't going to say, Dada, are you?"

"Mama mama."

"Mama is sleeping. Say Dada. I won't tell."

He blinks, shoves a hand in his mouth and sucks for a few seconds, then removes it again to say, "Da... ma. Mama."

"All right, that's good enough."

Dominick's head enters the frame as he leans in to kiss our son's face, whispering, "I love you."

And then, when the video ends, he turns the screen off

and returns his phone to his pocket while tears stream down my cheeks.

I don't even look up at him, turning toward him until I can bury my face in his chest and his arms are around me, holding me close in the way I know we've both ached for now.

"I watch that video every day and have since the day he died," he says into the top of my head, his voice hoarse. "I wanted to share it with you so many times…"

"I'm sorry," I whisper while lifting my head to look up into his grief-stricken face, knowing I don't have to apologize but doing so, anyway. "I was so caught up in my despair, I completely ignored yours. I just… just hated myself so much for not feeling connected to him."

"Shh." He strokes my hair and shakes his head. "I didn't show you to make you sad. I wanted you to see how much our son loved you, loved both of us. He was happy and loved and attached to you, even if you didn't feel like that was true."

I've never understood how he can, even in the middle of being emotional, remain rather calm compared to me. I push away from his chest and wipe the tears from my cheeks. "Aren't you angry?"

He slides his hands into his pant pockets and stares at me with his naturally dark and emotional eyes. "About what?"

"At the world. For Zander dying."

"I was at first." His gaze moves from mine to the shoreline. "Then it changed. I became more angry at not only losing my son, but losing you, too. One I had no control over, and the other, I've blamed myself endlessly for."

Wow. Hadn't expected that. Blinking, I step closer and wait for him to look back at me before asking, "Why don't you blame me?"

"Because you weren't well. You struggled from the moment he was born, and I didn't take it as seriously as I should have. I thought it was just new and everything, along with the lack of sleep for both of us. And if it wasn't, I figured you would tell me when it became too much. But you never said a word."

"Exactly. I never said anything, even though I knew something was wrong. I have some blame here."

He frowns. "I'm not blaming either of us. Just saying I noticed you were struggling and tried to help more, but it wasn't all you needed."

"You're right. It wasn't." This time, I'm the one to turn and stare out at the water. "Do you really want to do this again, Dominick?"

"If by 'do this' you mean to have a life with you, then the answer is 'yes.' Otherwise, I'm going to need you to clarify."

Of course, that's what I mean. "Aren't you afraid of...

of it happening again?" I don't have to elaborate; he knows what I'm asking.

"Terrified. But what has fear gotten either of us except separate lives without each other?"

"I didn't expect this." When he says nothing in response, I turn to him, and naturally, his gaze is focused on me. "As in, I thought we were over for good."

"I know. And I love you, Evie." He steps closer, lifting his hands to my face and leaning in, kissing my forehead as he murmurs, "I want nothing more than for you to give us another chance, and for both of us to push through our fear and try to have a family again."

"I don't know if I can."

The words come out of my mouth, but I know they aren't entirely accurate. I can. The thing is, I'm afraid of all the bad things happening again, and I've never been good at facing my fears.

"It will be hard for both of us," he says, tilting my face up so he's looking into my eyes before frowning. "It's difficult to admit it will be hard even for me, but we're stronger than this, Evie. It might not seem like we are, sweetheart, especially with everything that's happened, but we are."

I believe him, but only because I've changed a lot these past two years. I've dealt with things, I've lived on my own, and I did it all with no significant help. I'm stronger; surely I'm better equipped to handle tragedy now than before.

And so, for the first time in my life, I'll be fair to myself and the man I love. I'll push aside my fear and give our love another chance, because even though we lost our way for a while, walking away just doesn't feel right.

"I love you, too," I finally admit to him, enjoying the smile that lights up his face at hearing those words from me after so long, and then stop him from leaning in to kiss me with a few fingers over his lips. "But until I can tell Quinton what's happened to his face, that's all you'll get out of me."

"I didn't forget," he explains with a cheeky smirk, kissing my cheek after I remove my hand before dropping his own and stepping away. "But you can't blame me for trying."

No, I can't, and when he takes my hands in his again, interlacing our fingers, everything feels right between us for the first time since the day our son passed away.

CHAPTER 31

My father steps up next to where I stand at the railing on the porch the following afternoon, places one hand on my shoulder, and says with a definite smile in his voice, "Now you've got the same look in your eyes as him."

"I blame you for that."

"Good." He laughs at my teasing, his hand sliding off my shoulder to join the other on the railing as we both watch Dominick put the luggage in the car. "No reason for two people who love each other to remain apart."

I see the truth to his words now. I want to believe I would have acknowledged my feelings for Dominick eventually, but maybe not, because I didn't know what love truly entailed.

Now I know that Dominick embodies love. We both made mistakes, and will probably make more of them, but he always tried to make things right. He's cared for and loved me since the moment we met, and I fought against it because I didn't feel deserving of such care.

"Believing he loves me has always been the hardest part."

The admission is soft, and for a moment I don't think my father heard me, but then his hand covers mine on the railing. "You're not alone in that. Over the years, Colleen and I have had our moments, even nearly divorcing once. Nobody seems to tell you that difficulties are natural until you're already in trouble, but it's how you handle them that really matters."

"You're right, of course. I definitely didn't know, and neither of us were prepared for what happened."

"No, but you are now, and as long as you turn to each other, everything will be better than before."

Dominick shuts the car trunk then and turns back toward the house, smiling when he catches sight of us and stops when he reaches the top of the steps. "Ready?"

"No." My father replies first, and we all laugh as he pulls me into a bear hug. "Passed by too fast, but now we've got nothing except time. I'll be happy to have you anytime, both of you."

As he draws away, I wipe at my teary eyes while he shakes Dominick's hand, and then tell him, "I'll call you tomorrow."

"I'll be waiting."

Colleen comes out to say her goodbyes then, and a few

minutes later, we're headed back toward the airport and our changed lives once more.

❦

Dominick is unusually quiet on the trip home, even when driving me back to my apartment, which doesn't really bother me since I'm preoccupied with whether I should tell Quinton tonight or tomorrow before work.

When we arrive back at my place, Dom walks me to my door and carries my luggage inside, turning to face me after putting it down. "Talk tomorrow?"

"Yes, of course."

He nods and looks out the open door for a moment before grinning at me and lifting his hands to cradle my face.

"Dominick..."

I say his name as a warning, but it comes out breathless because my whole body hums with pleasure from his touch, as if the passion between us revived at the same time my feelings became clear again.

And he takes this moment to press his lips against mine, not with urgency, but a sweetness that makes tears spring to my eyes.

It only lasts a second before he draws away, drops his hands, and murmurs, "Until tomorrow, Evie."

Then, with that promise, he turns and leaves the apartment, shutting the door behind him with a soft click.

And once I get ahold of myself again, I grab my keys and head upstairs to end things with Quinton.

❧

Quinton opens the door with a happy smile, pulling me into a hug right there in the doorway before releasing me and stepping back to let me inside.

"Did you just get in?" He asks while shutting the door and turning to face me from where I've stopped just inside his place. "I didn't know you were returning so soon."

"Yeah, a little while ago." I clear my throat and jangle my keys in my pocket, staring at the floor for a second before lifting my gaze to his. "The trip was interesting."

"Oh?" He nods at the couch, his expression intrigued. "Want to have a seat? Need something to drink?"

"No, I can't stay long."

Now his expression changes to concern. "Everything okay?"

"Yes." I hate how emotional I am, especially as tears fill my eyes, but I've never had to break up with someone before. It's harder than I thought it would be, especially because of how he's looking at me. "My father was wonderful, and while there, I figured out a lot of things."

"I'm glad. I thought you might." He slips his hands into

his pockets with a soft chuckle, as smart as I know he is when he says, "That something you've figured out doesn't bode well for our relationship, does it?"

Even though that's exactly what it means, I wince and glance down at my feet. "I never made that apartment my home because it isn't. My home is with Dominick, and in my grief, I lost sight of everything. I believed I didn't love him because I didn't feel like I deserved it, especially not after feeling like I failed as a mother. I thought he should find someone better than me because of that."

"Hey." He steps closer and draws me into another hug, his chin resting on the top of my head as he says, "It's all right. I told you when you first started working with me that you had a friend in me. And as a friend, if you love him, then you should work things out with him. Nothing's changed between us, except I can't kiss you any longer, which is a tragedy, but I'll get over it."

He lets me go when I laugh at that, wiping at my tears with his thumbs while smiling at me. "That's better. And I know it won't make you feel less awful about breaking up with me, but you've helped me."

Trust Quinton to find the silver lining in all this. "I have?"

"Yes. I avoided dating until now. Will still be difficult as hell to put myself out there again, but I still want that house in the country, a white picket fence, two-and-a-half kids, and a dog. Oh, and can't forget the cat." He winks with that joking reminder of the day I agreed to go out with him for the first time. "See? I'll be fine."

"I know."

"Good. Now, go rest because there's a lot of work to do tomorrow and I'll need your help."

My answer is cheeky as I grab the keys out of my pocket. "Yes, sir. I'll see you at work in the morning."

He laughs and opens the door for me as he says, "Goodnight, Evie."

"Goodnight."

I stroll down the steps after the door clicks shut behind me, staring at my keys the entire time, and stop once in front of my apartment door.

Sticking the key in the lock, I open the door and stare at the apartment where I've spent the last two years of life, and the fact this place isn't my home is now impossible to ignore.

Not desiring to sleep here, I pick up my purse from the table by the door and grab my luggage so I at least have something to wear in the morning before locking up and getting into my car to head to the one place I'll always be welcome.

❧

Dominick opens his door after my second knock, grabbing my hand to tug me inside without a word, and shuts the door with his foot as he embraces me.

"It's official," I whisper to him while wrapping my arms around his neck and pressing a kiss to his neck. "I'm all yours."

"You always have been," he insists with a laugh, one of his hands traveling down my body until he cups my ass in his hands. "Let's go to bed."

"Yes, please. It's been a long day, and I'm exhausted."

He lifts me off the ground and carries me further inside with an exaggerated groan. "If you just want to sleep, I will have to spend the night on the couch."

"Hmm." I pretend to consider my options until he sets me down in the bedroom and shuts the door, enclosing us in darkness. "I have to be up in eight hours, and I need seven hours of sleep to function…"

He moves fast, cradling my face in his seconds before his mouth covers mine, and seeks entrance with a sweet sweep of his tongue.

Opening my mouth under his, I let him in, all while unbuttoning his shirt, and sliding my hands over his warm skin when it's finally bared to my touch.

Soon we're on the bed, skin-to-skin after a flurry of removing each other's clothing, his body covering mine while our locked lips share everything we feel.

It's passionate and familiar. Us.

And when our bodies join again for the first time in

two years, I hold on to him tight, every one of his thrusts bringing me closer to the edge. Every moment is beautiful, and when I fall apart in his arms, this man who will always help put me back together again falls apart in mine.

Our breathing evens out, but other than making sure he doesn't crush me, Dom doesn't move from above me, kissing my brow as he whispers, "I love you."

"I love you, too. And this, too," I say while wiggling beneath him.

He groans and rolls off with a soft laugh, bringing me with him until I'm lying on his chest, and kisses the top of my head. "I was actually going to talk to you about it tomorrow, but since you're here..."

"Hmm?"

"What do you think about moving? Starting over somewhere new?"

At that, I lift my head, and even though I can't see much of him in the dark, I know he's smiling. "I've never really thought about it. Where would we move?"

"Well, I'm certain I can find work anywhere, as can you, and seems to me you've got a lot of years to make up with your father, so close to him—" He doesn't even get to finish his sentence before I cut him off with a kiss. When I finally let him up for air, he chuckles. "I assume that's a yes."

"Are you kidding? That's a hell yes. I... I would love it."

"I'm glad." He grins, cradling my cheek gently. "You'll

have your family and a support system, and... if and when you're ready, maybe us having another child won't seem so daunting then."

He says it with so much hope and sweetness that suddenly I feel the need to reassure him. "When I said yes to giving us another chance, I meant all of it, Dom. I'm wary, I think both of us would be foolish not to be, but overall, I'm optimistic. I don't want fear deciding anything for us ever again."

Instead of responding with words, he slides his hand around to the back of my neck and brings my mouth to his for another few slow and deep kisses. Then he withdraws and says, "Hold on. One more thing."

He rolls me over until I'm on my back once more before leaving the bed and walking over to his dresser. I can't see what he's doing, other than the fact he's opening a drawer, but then he's back and lying next to me.

Yawning, I cover my mouth and stare at him through the darkness. "What's the one more thing?"

"I think we've forgotten something important."

"Such as the fact I've got to be up in seven hours now and need to sleep?"

"I know," he says while grabbing my left hand and holding it in his. "Say you'll marry me again, Evie, and I'll stop talking so you can rest."

My smile, even though he probably can't see it, is broad and bright in the darkness. "Of course, I will."

I feel him slide a ring onto my finger and at my gasp, he lies back down beside me and snuggles me from behind with a whispered, "Goodnight, sweetheart."

The moment, although so different from the first time I agreed to become his wife, is perfect for where we are now.

And when I close my eyes, finally drifting off to sleep, there's no doubt in my mind that I'll ever let the man I love go ever again.

EPILOGUE

"Dada!" Emily, our fourteen-month-old daughter, squeals as Dominick finally walks in the door, toddling over to him as fast as her little feet will take her. "Up!"

He removes his coat and shoes before giving her exactly what she wants, picking up and holding her in the air for a brief second before bringing her down for a kiss.

Then, he smiles at me while placing her on his shoulders, her little legs kicking excitedly because she loves being up there, but my father speaks first.

"About time you got here," he says with a laugh. "We were afraid the snow finally defeated you."

"Are you kidding? I'm a pro at driving in snow by now." He casts me a hopeful glance. "Please tell me I didn't miss dinner because I'm starving."

"As if we would ever let you go hungry," Colleen

announces as she walks in the room. "Now you just give me that little sweetie and grab yourself a plate."

Emily switches from Dom's shoulders to Colleen's arms with glee, babbling the whole time, and I follow him into the kitchen.

He doesn't miss a beat, trapping me against the counter in our kitchen and kissing me until we're both breathless, clinging to one another as if we haven't seen each other in a week.

Only, unlike usual, we actually haven't this time.

"Remind me to take you to any conferences with me in the future."

"That bad, huh?"

"Awful." He moves away and takes a plate out of the nearby cupboard, putting some food on it before shoving it in the microwave. "Not to mention, I almost missed my flight, and then we sat on the runway for an hour after the initial take off time. I swore if I missed Christmas, I would quit my job on the spot."

I don't even try to hide my laughter. "So dramatic. It's only Christmas Eve, and Emily doesn't understand time yet, so if we had to postpone opening presents, she wouldn't have any idea."

"I would, however." The microwave beeps, so he opens the door and sticks his finger in the mashed potatoes, then shakes his head and shuts the door again to heat it up longer. "Did you get everything wrapped?"

"I did. Well, all the gifts except one."

The microwave beeps again. "I can do it," he offers while opening up the door and pulling out his plate, cursing as he places the hot plate on the counter and closes the door again. "You think I would know better at my age and let the dish cool down for a second."

"You'd think." Smiling, I step forward and slide a hand through his wet hair. Then, grabbing the front of his shirt, I step up on tiptoe and give him another quick kiss. "I missed you. It's freezing here in the wintertime, especially in bed."

He clears his throat and peeks over my shoulder to make sure we're still alone before making me squeal by grabbing my ass and murmuring, "Oh, don't worry, I'll make it up to you later."

"Lucky me."

He winks and picks up his plate, carrying it over to the table, and patting the seat beside him. As I sit down, how word has changed into something positive is amazing.

Within six months after becoming re-engaged, we married a second time, and my father got to walk me down the aisle. A month before the wedding, we purchased this house and moved in. It was less than five miles from my father's house and perfect for raising a family in, something we waited on until we became settled into our new life together.

We both found new jobs — Quinton had been sad to

see me go, but understood — and for a while, it was just me and Dominick enjoying the time we got to spend with each other. We also spent plenty of quality time with my father and Colleen, and William when he was around.

Then... well, I ended up pregnant with Emily, and all the terrifying feelings resurfaced the instant the test came back positive. I tried not to focus on it, both Dominick and I struggled with all the what-ifs the entire time, but when they laid her on my chest, it wasn't anything like before.

My baby and I were connected, and yes, for a little while, I would compulsively check to make sure she was still breathing, but we've made it just fine.

And I am lucky. For love and a second chance at marriage and children with Dom and for everything else I appreciate in a way I never could before.

So when he finishes eating, rinses off his plate, and turns to me to ask, "Where's this present that isn't wrapped?" there's only one way to answer his question.

I step forward, grab his hand, and watch his eyes widen as I place it against my stomach while my lips curve upward in a mischievous smile, telling him everything he needs to know.

For us, it's another happy beginning in a series of new beginnings, with a love that will see us through whatever happens as long as we have each other.

THE END

Thanks for reading! I hope you enjoyed the happy ending to Evie's story. If so, please consider telling your friends or posting a short review on the site you purchased this book from. Word of mouth is an author's best friend and much appreciated!

ABOUT THE AUTHOR

Violet Haze is a big fan of writing and reading romance. The autistic mother of one, she currently spends her days writing, reading, procrastinating, playing violin and learning guitar, & listening to her son play video games she doesn't understand.

For information on other books to read, including links to ALL the vendors, visit her website:
www.authorviolethaze.com

Want to contact Violet?
Email her at: violet@authorviolethaze.com

www.ingramcontent.com/pod-product-compliance
Lightning Source LLC
Chambersburg PA
CBHW021657110726
47902CB00007B/1972